KU-013-838

to Mum, Dad, and Gramps,
for all the stories

KIKI KALLIRA

BREAKS A KINGDOM

SANGU
MANDANNA

HODDER CHILDREN'S BOOKS

First published in Great Britain in 2021 by Hodder & Stoughton
First published in the United States in 2021 by Viking, an imprint of
Penguin Random House LLC

1 3 5 7 9 10 8 6 4 2

Text copyright © Sangu Mandanna, 2021
Illustrations copyright © Nabi H. Ali, 2021

The moral rights of the author and illustrator have been asserted.

*All characters and events in this publication, other than those clearly
in the public domain, are fictitious and any resemblance to real persons,
living or dead, is purely coincidental.*

All rights reserved.
No part of this publication may be reproduced, stored in a retrieval system,
or transmitted, in any form or by any means, without the prior permission in
writing of the publisher, nor be otherwise circulated in any form of binding or
cover other than that in which it is published and without a similar condition
including this condition being imposed on the subsequent purchaser.

A CIP catalogue record for this book is available from the British Library.

ISBN 978 1 444 96344 1

Typeset in Casus Pro by Jouve (UK), Milton Keynes
Printed and bound in Great Britain by Clays Ltd, Elcograf S.p.A.

The paper and board used in this book
are made from wood from responsible sources.

Hodder Children's Books
An imprint of
Hachette Children's Group
Part of Hodder & Stoughton Limited
Carmelite House
50 Victoria Embankment
London EC4Y 0DZ

An Hachette UK Company
www.hachette.co.uk

www.hachettechildrens.co.uk

THE CAST

ASHWINI: The heroine of Kiki's drawings. Fierce, proud and brave, she is an Asura slayer and the leader of a group of rebel kids (the Crows).

ASURA: A huge, monstrous demon from Hindu folklore.

BRAHMA: An incredibly powerful god from Hindu folklore. Brahma is the god of creation.

CHAMUNDESHWARI: An incredibly powerful goddess from Hindu folklore. She once rode into battle on the back of her great lion and defeated Mahishasura in a long, bitter fight.

JOJO: A member of the group of rebel kids (the Crows). Jojo is a tailor and the Crow's archer.

KRITIKA 'KIKI' KALLIRA: A creator and worrier. Armed with her pencil, Kiki is pulled into the mystical world she has drawn.

LEJ: A member of the group of rebel kids (the Crows). Lej finds whatever the Crows need, whatever it takes.

MAHISHASURA: The cruellest and most powerful of all the Asuras. He is a buffalo demon and the king of Asuras. No god or man can kill him. He has been banished to a realm between worlds (the Nowhere Place).

PIP: A member of the group of rebel kids (the Crows). When Kiki was little, Pip was her imaginary friend and companion on endless adventures. Pip is the very first of Kiki's creations.

SAMARA: A member of the group of rebel kids (the Crows). Samara *loves* books and does research for the Crows.

SIMHA: Chamundeshwari's enormous, talking lion. He is a fighter and a fusser and drinks tea out of a ludicrously tiny cup. Simha means 'lion' in Kannada – a language spoken in several regions of South West India.

SUKI: A member of the group of rebel kids (the Crows). Suki is the Crow's apothecary.

VISHNU: An incredibly powerful god from Hindu folklore. Vishnu is the god of preservation.

1

I had absolutely, definitely killed my mother.

OK, maybe not *definitely*, but I was pretty sure of it. Like ninety per cent sure. Maybe eight-five.

It all depended on whether I had locked the front door when I left our house earlier today, and no matter how hard I tried, I couldn't remember if I had. And if I *hadn't*, well, then there was a very good chance that Mum, who had been repainting the kitchen cabinets when I left, had since been murdered by a burglar.

Or had been eaten by an opportunistic goose, which only sounds ridiculous if you haven't met the geese that live in London.

The day hadn't started on such a tragic note. It was a hot July, and school had just finished for the summer, so I left home right after lunch to meet my best friend

Emily, her little sister Tam and two of Tam's friends. We took the bus halfway across the city to one of those pop-up amusement parks that always appear in the summer. We'd planned it for weeks and it was awesome at first. We had eaten ice creams in the sunshine, taken turns go-karting and tried to win those giant cuddly teddy bears.

We had just joined the queue for the Ferris wheel when Tam said something about a locked room in a mystery book she was reading, and it had suddenly occurred to me that I couldn't remember if I'd locked my front door.

Now I bit restlessly on the end of my thumb and screwed my forehead up as I tried, once *again*, to remember. I could picture myself stepping out of the front door, and I could kind of picture myself putting my silver key in the silver keyhole in the door, but was I remembering that from *today* or was I just remembering it from the gazillions of *other* times I had locked the door?

'Kiki?' Emily gave me a gentle jab with her elbow. 'You OK?'

I nodded and tried to concentrate on what she and the others were saying, but all I could think about was

2

the front door of my house. As far as I was concerned, the sequence of hypothetical consequences of an unlocked front door went something like this: burglar (or goose) sees unlocked front door; burglar (or goose) can't believe their good luck; burglar (or goose) bumps into Mum while attempting to loot the kitchen; and then, inevitably, burglar (or goose) murders (or eats) Mum.

Emily's eyes moved to my hand, and she watched with concern as I mauled my thumbnail. 'You're not OK,' she said, and lowered her voice so that Tam and Tam's friends wouldn't hear her. 'What's up?'

If it had been anyone other than Emily or Mum, I would have lied and pretended I felt sick or had a headache or something, but it *was* Emily, so I told her the truth.

And because she was Emily, she listened to me and then she nodded. 'And it won't matter if I tell you that your mother's death by goose is extremely unlikely, will it? Because once it's in your head, you can't get it out?'

She knew me so well.

'I should go home and check the door,' I said. Shame, anger and frustration made me grit my teeth.

'If I don't, I'll just spend the rest of the day worrying about it.'

'OK, I'll come with you.'

'No!' I said at once. 'Stay. I'll just feel worse if you leave, too.'

Emily hesitated, but then she said, 'My mum's making Chinese chicken stew for dinner tonight. Come over and eat with us?'

'Chinese *ginger* chicken stew?' I asked, perking up.

Emily grinned. 'Yep.'

So after promising her that I would go to hers for dinner, I left the park in slightly better spirits. On the bus ride home, I pulled my feet up on to the seat, took my overstuffed sketchbook out of my backpack and sketched a quick doodle of the Ferris wheel. I drew Emily's tiny delighted face peeping out of the car at the very top, and then mine next to hers. I giggled to myself as I added a gull in the sky above us, pooping on Emily's head. She'd love that when I showed her later.

I lowered my pencil and just looked at the sketch for a moment. Seeing the miniature version of me looking so happy on the Ferris wheel made me feel a little like I hadn't missed out after all. And on top of that, the twenty minutes I had spent on the sketch was twenty minutes I hadn't been thinking about my front door.

But when I got home and discovered that the front door *was* locked, all the warm, fuzzy feelings the doodle had given me dissolved as quickly as a lump of sugar in hot tea. I could see my blurry reflection in the panes of frosted glass in the door, so I just glared at her, the other me. I was furious with myself. I'd left a fun day out with my best friend because I hadn't been able to stop obsessing about a *door*.

I let myself into the house quietly, resisting the temptation to slam the door in question. I could have gone back to the amusement park, I suppose, but then Tam and her friends would think I was even stupider than they probably already did.

As far as I could tell, becoming obsessed with a stray thought or fear, to the point that I couldn't *not* act on it, was not something most people did. But I couldn't help it. I knew I had been all sunshine and fearlessness when I was little, but at some point, anxiousness had crept up on me. I got twitchy about all sorts of stuff now. I worried the spider that ran under the floorboard would reappear on my pillow. I worried a shark would sneak into my school's swimming pool (and, yes, I *did* actually know how absurd that sounded, but I worried about it anyway). I worried that a random, inconsequential thing I had said three days before was actually quite a stupid thing to say, and maybe everyone who heard it was now convinced *I* was stupid. I worried that Mum wouldn't come home one day. I worried that one of us had forgot to close the kitchen window before bed—

And so on.

I guess it wouldn't be so bad if all I did was feel anxious for a little while, but that was never the end of it. Nope. I had to *do* something about it, or else I would never be able to get the worry or thought out of my head. That didn't matter so much when it was stuff like the spider, because Mum would come to my room, find it, and poof! The worrying would stop, just like that. But sometimes it wasn't quite that easy. Sometimes it was a lot harder to get my brain to be quiet again.

As I hung my backpack up on the hook in the hallway, the faint smell of paint and the sound of happy pop music drifted out of the kitchen, followed by Mum's perfectly alive voice: 'Kiki? Is that you?'

I stuck my head in the kitchen, where she was painting the last of the cupboards. There were yellow splatters on her clothes, her hands, even on her dark hair, which was exactly like mine apart from the fact that hers was cut below her chin in a pretty bob and mine was longer and almost always up in a ponytail. I would have liked a bob, too, but I knew that if I didn't have my hair pulled away from my face and hands, I would never stop fidgeting with it, tucking it behind my ears, twirling it around a finger, all that. I already bit my fingernails every time I saw even a little of the white end-part grow back, so I really didn't need another distracting bad habit.

'You look like lemon pie,' I informed my mother, giggling. I snatched her phone off the counter and took a photo of her.

'Horrid thing,' she said affectionately. '*You* picked this colour.'

'It's nice on the cupboards, but pretty weird on a human.'

With a look in her eye I could only describe as evil, she flicked the wide paintbrush in my direction. I squealed as splotches of cold yellow paint sprayed my cheek and shoulder.

'You're right,' she said, grinning, 'it *does* look pretty weird on a human.'

She was the actual worst. I grinned back.

'So,' she went on, tossing me a tea towel to dab the paint off my face, 'why are you back so early?'

'Oh, I couldn't remember if I'd locked the front door and I was pretty sure you'd been eaten by a goose, so I came back to check.'

It was the truth, but I said it cheerfully, like it was silly and funny. Mum knew about the anxiousness, the obsessions, the need to *do* something. She was always nice about it and never made me feel bad, not even that time last year when I woke her at four in the morning by leaning over her to make sure she was still breathing. She just said, 'Well, I used to do it to you when you were a baby, so I guess this is payback,' and let me sleep in her bed for the rest of the night.

But I didn't think Mum knew just how bad it was for me. I had never told her, so how could she? It wasn't that I didn't want to. I just didn't want to worry her.

And I guess maybe I also didn't want to tell her because that would make this A Big Deal. A Giant Something. I didn't want it to be Something. I wanted it to be Nothing; irrelevant, unimportant. I wanted it to be a Nothing that didn't disrupt my life, or make me unhappy, or turn me into someone I didn't even know any more. A Nothing so unimportant, it would go away very soon, and I'd get the sunshiny version of me back.

Now, narrowing her eyes at me, Mum ignored my nonsense about geese and cut right to the important part: 'You were so worried about whether you'd locked the front door that you left your friends early and came all the way back?'

I didn't want to lie to her, so I tiptoed around it by saying, 'Well, and I felt a little sick. It was really hot.' Both true.

'Kiki—'

'Oh!' I said excitedly, shamelessly interrupting her before the conversation became Something. 'You'll never believe what Emily told me today! Her mum is going to have another baby.'

Just like that, Mum was distracted. It was cool that Emily was going to have a baby brother or another sister, but I wasn't really all that interested in babies. Mum, on the other hand, *loved* babies. I was pretty sure she'd have had at least five of her own if my dad hadn't died before I was born.

'A new baby!' Mum cooed. 'Hand me my phone, will you, duckling? I'll text Mei and see if she needs anything.'

'Can I look through your stash of blank notebooks while you're on the phone? I've run out of space in my sketchbook.'

'Yes, of course.'

I left her excitedly tapping out a text to Emily's mum, and went upstairs to the room Mum used as her home office. She worked in animation, so she usually went to a studio to work with a team of other animators on a project, but she also did some teaching and tried to work from home whenever she could. Which meant her home office got a lot of use and was filled with student essays, storyboards, piles of research materials, her shiny computer monitor and graphics tablet, and her bookshelves, including an entire shelf crammed with empty notebooks and sketchpads.

I edged around a stack of books to get to the shelf. I picked up the one on top – *The Illustrated Book of Indian Folklore: Vol. I*, a beautiful, enormous thing Mum had read to me when I was little. And, yes, it was only volume one, because it turned out there was a *lot* of Indian folklore. Stories of monsters and gods and heroes, of goddesses who rode lions, of demons who kidnapped princesses, of kings and queens and cities and snarky jackals and, well, a whole lot more than that, too.

I'd loved those stories. They'd been special to Mum, stories she'd grown up with in Karnataka, in the south of India, where she'd spent half her life before moving here.

After putting *The Illustrated Book of Indian Folklore: Vol. I* back on the stack of books, I checked the shelf of empty notebooks. There were a few that would do the trick, but I kept looking for The One. Like a warrior choosing her sword or a witch choosing her wand, I, Kiki Kallira, had to choose my new sketchbook. It was not a task to be taken lightly. The wrong choice could prove to be the undoing of the universe!

And then I found it. It was beautiful, bound in white spirals, with two hundred thick sheets of clean white art paper. The cover was a perfect, soft buttery yellow, the exact colour of evening sunshine.

It had been so nice and uncomplicated to be a sunshine girl. Not so long ago, I had found it easy to fall asleep at night. I hadn't needed to search the whole house just because I'd seen a shadow out of the corner of my eye, and never got a scratchy feeling inside my brain when a book on a shelf had its spine facing in. Why wasn't I like that any more?

Maybe this *was* Something, after all. I knew this wasn't normal, but I couldn't help feeling like it was all my fault for not being stronger and braver. Why else would this anxiousness, this Something, sneak in and make itself so completely at home?

My eyes had filled with tears and I was clutching the yellow sketchbook so tightly my knuckles had gone white, so I turned quickly and went across the landing to my bedroom. Flopping down on to my rug with my box of art supplies, I opened my new sketchbook and started to draw the first thing that popped into my mind.

Monsters started to take shape on the first page. First the wolf from *Little Red Riding Hood*, then the Beast from *Beauty and the Beast*, and then an Asura – a huge, monstrous demon from Indian folklore. By the time I'd finished the pencil outline of the Asura, I felt calmer.

No, it was even better than that: as I stared at that third sketch, I felt the sudden, electric excitement you get when you have a totally brilliant idea.

One of the stories Mum had told me years ago, with my bedside lamp turned down low and *The*

Illustrated Book of Indian Folklore on her lap, was the story of the Asura king Mahishasura. It went something like this:

Hundreds of years ago, long before India became the country it is now, there was a kingdom in the south called Mysore. It was a rich, golden city, with beautiful shining palaces, gentle hills, and lush green land.

Then Mahishasura came to Mysore. He was the cruelest and most powerful of all the Asuras. He killed the kings of Mysore and took the city for himself. The people resisted, but they were no match for him or his Asura army. They stole children from their beds, burnt the crops and threw anyone who tried to fight back into deep prisons so that they never saw the sun again. And Mysore became a sad, dark place, where the people lived in fear and where all hope seemed lost.

The first question I'd asked when Mum told me the story was, 'But why didn't the gods stop him?'

In Indian folklore, the gods are always incredibly powerful, and three of them in particular: Brahma, the creator; Vishnu, the preserver; and Shiva, the destroyer. When I'd pointed this out to Mum, she rolled her eyes and said, 'If you keep your gob closed for longer than two seconds, Kiki, you might find out.'

Because, as it turned out, Mahishasura had a secret weapon. Before he came to Mysore, he had spent years praying to Brahma. Impressed with his persistence (and I guess because gods did this kind of thing all the time in the stories), Brahma had offered him a boon.

'I want to be immortal,' Mahishasura said.

'I can't do that,' Brahma replied. 'All I can do is make you so powerful that no god or man can kill you.'

Satisfied, Mahishasura accepted the gift. No god or man could kill him.

So when the whole destroying-Mysore thing happened, the gods were a *teensy* bit annoyed. They went to Brahma and demanded to know how they were supposed to defeat Mahishasura while he was protected by such a powerful boon.

'Well,' said Brahma, 'I said no god or man could kill him. Perhaps you should send a goddess.'

So the gods combined their power and created the warrior goddess Chamundeshwari, who was every bit as awesome as she sounded. She rode into Mysore on the back of a great lion and, at the foot of the hills, she and Mahishasura had a long, bitter battle. In the end, she won. She killed the demon king and saved Mysore. Yay!

To show her how grateful they were, the people of Mysore gave the hills a new name in her honour. They called them the Chamundi Hills. ('The next time we visit Granny and Gramps,' Mum said, 'I'll take you to Mysore to see the real Chamundi Hills. You can even see a statue of Mahishasura and a temple for Chamundeshwari at the top!')

It was a fun story. Just a story. Much like Zeus and Thor and Osiris, Mahishasura had never *really* existed. I sometimes liked to think they had all been around once, because mythology was so cool, but I was eleven years old and I kind of knew myths were just myths. Jackals didn't talk, the sun wasn't pulled across the sky by a god in a chariot, and Asuras weren't real.

And the totally amazing idea I had right then, with the yellow sketchbook open in front of me, was to create a Kiki version of the old city of Mysore and retell the story of Mahishasura my own way.

I sketched quick, sharp lines with my pencil, went over them in black ink and filled the shapes in with shades of cream, white, gold and red. Mysore Palace sparkled back at me from the paper, almost exactly like the one I had seen in the real city the last time Mum and I visited India. It was so warm and alive that

I could almost hear the birds and feel the heat of the sun.

I drew outwards from there, taking pieces out of the story Mum had told me and jumbling them up with my own whimsical ideas. I drew palaces and clockwork trains, outdoor markets and rainbow houses. Red London double-decker buses and jackals in deep, dark woods. Cobblestone streets and lush green hills. A circus that never stopped, a castle in the sky. Sketch after sketch after sketch. Black ink and vivid colours. My hand cramped and my neck ached, but I barely noticed because I was so excited about the world growing right in front of me. *My* world.

I'd been having so much fun with my weird, perfect, patchwork Mysore that I didn't really want to ruin it by introducing Mahishasura and his army of demons into it. But all good stories need an enemy the heroes have to fight, right?

I started with his head. Mahishasura was a buffalo demon, so I drew a pair of thick, curled horns. It took me a little while to get the pencil lines just right, but once I was happy with them, I inked them in with bold, black strokes.

And that was when the real world got weird.

At first, it just felt like I was on a train. A bit rumbly, but fine. Then the rumble got rumblier and my whole bedroom shook. I looked up in time to see an empty cup rattle violently on my desk. My coloured pencils rolled away from me. The cup crashed to the floor.

The sky outside my window went dark. Not night-time dark, but the dark of storm clouds. They gathered and swept across the sky, churning in time to the rumble of the earth.

Somewhere below, Mum's voice called my name in alarm. I looked out of the window and saw that beyond our back garden, the river was choppy and frothy, like the waves on an ocean. A boat rocked back and forth while water splashed over the tall sides of the riverbank.

Then, abruptly, it stopped. Just like that. The room went still, the skies cleared, the sun came back out and the river went quiet.

'Kiki?' Mum was out of breath as she appeared in the doorway of my room. 'Are you OK?'

'What *was* that?'

'An earthquake, I think,' she said, perplexed.

Of course, it hadn't been an earthquake at all, but we didn't know that then. We didn't know that the

17

furious churning of the earth, water and sky had been a warning.

This was the point at which I should have thrown my beautiful yellow sketchbook into the river, but I didn't know that, either. Instead, I threw away the broken cup, made myself a cheese toastie and kept drawing.

2

Fast forward three months to October. Emily and I went back to school, Emily's mum told us the new baby was going to be a boy and my not-so-new-any-more sketchbook was almost full.

'Kiki?'

It was Mum's voice, but I didn't answer her. I was in the middle of a really detailed, delicate sketch of one of my characters' battles with an Asura and I just *couldn't* stop now, not when the strokes of my pencil were coming so quickly and I was *so* close to capturing the look of glee on my heroine's face.

'Kiki!'

A swoop of my pencil for the swish of her hair as she leaped at the Asura, a sword shining in her hand.

'Kritika. Kallira.'

Uh-oh. Mum had used The Voice *and* my full name.

I tore my eyes away from the paper. 'Yes?'

'Come down here, please!' she called, clearly exasperated. 'Granny and Gramps want to say hi.'

With one last mournful look at my sketchbook, I left it behind on my bed. It had been a few days since we'd last FaceTimed with my grandparents and I did really like talking to them, but I just wished it didn't have to be right *now*.

'She never has her nose out of that book,' Mum was saying as I walked down the stairs.

'Oh my word,' Granny's voice replied somewhat drily, 'I wonder who she gets that from.'

Mum snorted a laugh, but said, 'I don't think I'm *quite* as bad.' I could almost picture her shaking her head. 'I love that Kiki is so passionate about something and works so hard at it, and her art really is brilliant, but I wish she'd spend a little more time in the real world.'

But the real world was so much harder to live in.

I went into the kitchen. 'Hi, Granny! Hi, Gramps!'

'There you are, pet!' Gramps boomed from the screen of the tablet propped up on the kitchen counter. 'It's always lovely to see your smile.'

Granny stuck her head into the frame as well. 'A few of your aunties are here,' she said. I noticed she was wearing a sari, which was unusual. 'I think they want to say hello, too.'

Then there was a flurry as Granny and Gramps got out of the way, and three beaming, plump aunties pushed and jostled each other to get a good look at me.

'Kritika!' one of them squealed. Her hands flapped at me like she was dying to pinch my cheeks. I could practically feel the bruises forming. 'Look at you! Eleven years old now, hmm? You look more and more like Ashwini thayi every year.'

'Every year,' another auntie echoed. 'If you turn your face just slightly to the right, Kritika, you could be a replica of that old photo of Ashwini thayi!'

Ashwini thayi was our family's cautionary tale. *Thayi* means grandmother, but it can be used for pretty much any female relative who is either dead or old. Ashwini had been my great-grandmother's sister and she had died at the age of thirteen, of causes that no one could ever agree on because no one who had actually known her was still alive. Gramps said it was the flu (which was probably true), my uncle Shiv said it was a broken heart (what?) and at least five different distantly related aunties all insisted it had been bad behaviour (again, what?).

So the kids in the family were all pretty used to hearing things like, 'Careful, or you'll end up like Ashwini thayi!' or 'Do you want to end up like Ashwini thayi? No? Then don't be so cheeky!'

I always felt like poor Ashwini thayi deserved a better story than that, so I had put a version of her in my Mysore. Honestly, my version of her was no truer to the real Ashwini than the stories the aunties came out with, but I liked to think she would have liked it. My Ashwini was an Asura slayer; fierce, proud and brave. In my Mysore, Ashwini thayi got to be a hero.

Coincidentally, she was the one I had been drawing when Mum interrupted me.

The aunties were still talking over one another. I caught snatches of, 'How are you?' and 'What are you studying in school these days?' and then, at last, Granny wrestled her phone back and shooed them away.

'Are you having a party?' I asked her, puzzled by the unusual number of visitors in their house this late in the day. India was four and a half hours ahead of us, so it was past ten o'clock at night there.

'Only a small one,' said Granny. 'It's Dussehra.'

Dussehra is an Indian festival. It was celebrated in different ways around the country, but in Karnataka, the state where my grandparents lived, it was celebrated with lots of delicious food, elephant parades in cities like Mysore, and processions of goddess statues down the river Kaveri. Part of the festival was about celebrating Chamundeshwari's defeat of the demon king Mahishasura.

The Kodava people of Coorg, which was where Gramps's family came from and where Ashwini thayi used to live, celebrated the actual Kaveri instead. Their beliefs revolved around the river and our ancestors rather than gods or goddesses, so their Dussehra sometimes involved a trip to Talakaveri, the place where the river begins.

Basically, India has a *lot* of different traditions and cultures, probably because there was a time not so long ago when the country was a bunch of separate states and kingdoms. I didn't even know most of the traditions, but I was pretty sure people in the north of the country celebrated Dussehra differently. They called Chamundeshwari by the name Durga, for a start, and in some places, their Dussehra celebrated the defeat of a totally different demon king by a totally different god instead.

Mum and I usually went to India once a year, during the summer, but one time, we went in October, and that was the only time I'd ever celebrated Dussehra myself. It had been a whole week of eating delicious things, which, as far as I was concerned, made it the best festival ever. Sometimes, if I tried really hard, I could almost still taste some of the treats we'd had: Mysore pak, a buttery, sugary biscuit that came in slabs; jalebis, those sweet, sticky, sunset-coloured rings soaked in syrup; dosas, which were sort of like savoury crepes that I'd slather with butter; and kaju katlis, diamond-shaped sweets made out of ground-up cashews and sugar.

There had been a *lot* of sugar involved. I was practically drooling just thinking about it now.

'I'm so jealous,' I said mournfully.

'I'll eat an extra piece of kaju katli just for you,' Gramps said generously.

'I have a whole box of Mysore pak right here,' Granny chimed in, a very Mum-esque twinkle of mischief in her eye. 'Do you want to see?'

Mum and I looked at each other in a moment of

mutual sorrow that we'd been saddled with a family like this.

After the call, Mum started chopping garlic and onions for the risotto she was making us for dinner. As I measured out the rice, she said, 'Kiki, I know you overheard what I said to Granny and Gramps about your art ...'

'Would that be the part where you said I'm brilliant?' I asked, smiling angelically.

She rolled her eyes. 'I know what it's like to love something so much that you hate to be parted from it. I could read books and scribble with my pencil all day.'

'I'd do that, too, but I'd also need cake,' I said firmly.

She considered that. 'Same, actually.' And then she gave herself a quick shake. 'The point is, it's OK to love the worlds inside your head.'

'But?'

'No, that's it,' she said, and smiled. 'It's OK. Yes, it's annoying when I have to yell your name six times before you hear me but, you know, pot and kettle. If this is what makes you feel better on a bad day, then I'm glad you have it.'

Guilt and love and gratitude made my throat tight, so I just hugged her. I had never told her how bad it got sometimes inside my brain, but maybe I didn't need to. She understood me anyway. She *got* me.

Later, teeth brushed and pyjamas on, I went back to my room and, more importantly, back to my sketchbook. Ashwini took shape on the clean white paper; a girl with a sharp dark bob, merry brown eyes, a red leather jacket and an expression of pure glee on her face as she battled one of Mahishasura's demon soldiers.

In my story, Ashwini was the leader of a group of rebel kids who were trying to take Mysore back from the Asuras. They called themselves the Crows, because crows are stubborn and cunning and loyal, and they lived in a lovely crooked house that had a talent for hiding them from Mahishasura's minions.

The crooked house wasn't going to be in this sketch, though. I wasn't sure what the background would be yet, but it would be outdoors, maybe on a large arched bridge over the Kaveri.

I sketched out the finer details of the Asura that Ashwini was fighting. He was a dragon demon, like the one the god Indra had defeated in one of the myths, and he was the size of a horse, with enormous black wings, slit nostrils that breathed smoke, a spiky scarlet tongue and shiny black jewels for scales. Before Ashwini had tracked him down, he had been one of Mahishasura's most feared minions. The sight of his silhouette swooping across the night sky had made the people of Mysore tremble in fear.

I inked over the pale pencil lines and reached for my box of coloured pencils. Sweeping black lines and blocks of rich colour transformed the white paper into something alive. Soon, the battle felt so real that I could almost feel the hiss of the Asura's breath on my face.

My bed gave a jerk beneath me. I jerked, too, startled.

'Hello?' I said foolishly.

Funnily enough, no one answered.

I shrugged it off and went back to my sketch. I gave the Asura's tail a wicked curve.

'Ow!'

I dropped the pencil and snatched my hands back. It had been a quick, sudden burst of pain, like an electric shock. I could have sworn it had come from my sketchbook!

After a moment of hesitation, I put one hand back down on the page, ready to snatch it away if I needed to. Nothing happened. It was just paper. *My* paper, as much a part of me as my own skin.

I was probably just tired. It had been a while since I'd had more than five or six hours of sleep at night, and while it was *definitely* more fun to stay up and draw than it was to stay up wondering if I needed to double-check the downstairs windows, I knew I'd be useless at school tomorrow if I didn't at least try to sleep.

I put my sketchbook and pencils back on my desk, got under my warm, cuddly blanket and flicked my lamp off.

When I woke up, my desk was in flames and there was a demon in my bedroom.

3

These were just implausible levels of bad luck. I had bad dreams just like everybody else, of course, but it seemed a little unfair that this dream involved a demon *and* a fire. Just one of the two would have been more than enough, thanks.

I stayed calm. I sat up, blinked at the demon and tried to ignore how real the heat from the flames felt.

The Asura regarded me silently. He was exactly like the one I had drawn before I fell sleep. Black-jewel scales, slit nostrils with curls of smoke and malevolent eyes. I swallowed. It was fine to be a little scared at this point, right? Even if you knew it wasn't real?

'Can I help you?' I asked politely.

The Asura narrowed those eyes. 'What is this place?' he demanded. His voice was a low snarl.

Tiny beads of sweat formed on the tip of my nose. The room had become hot and smoky.

'This is London,' I said.

'Lun-din,' the Asura repeated, testing the syllables in his mouth. 'Not Mysore?'

'No ... ?'

'Then he did it,' the Asura rumbled. Was that wonder in his voice? 'Mahishasura has found a way home at last.'

This didn't sound like good news to me.

'Kiki? What's all that noise down there?'

The Asura whipped around at the sound of Mum's voice from her bedroom in the loft above us. As he did, his wickedly sharp tail hit my leg, where blood bloomed immediately.

'Ow!'

This was the second time I had said that tonight. I stared at the blood, while the flames from the desk spread to the window curtains, and I felt a sudden, horrible terror.

This wasn't a dream, was it?

I did not stay calm. Even as my brain rejected the possibility that this was real, my body started to panic. My heart pounded. My curtains were on fire, my desk was on fire, *the sketchbook on my desk was on fire.*

And the Asura was gone.

I heard a crash from downstairs as the front door slammed open. He had escaped.

Great. There was a demon loose in London.

'What was that?' I could hear Mum shifting in bed. She would be downstairs any minute now. 'Was that the door?'

There was literally no way I could answer that honestly, so I lied. 'I didn't hear anything!' I squeaked.

What was I supposed to deal with first? Fire or demon? Demon or fire?

Well, one of the two was still in my house with my mother, so that settled things. Holding my breath and scrunching up my eyes to block out as much smoke as I could, I dragged my blankets off my bed, smacked at the curtains with them and then threw them over the desk to smother the remaining flames.

Then I turned and ran, barefoot, out of my room, down the stairs and out of the open front door. I had absolutely no idea what I planned to do when I found the Asura, who was an impressively ferocious dragony demony *thing* while I was just a kid in her favourite pyjamas, but I couldn't just let him get away, either. After all, I was the one who had somehow set him loose.

Not to mention the fact that he was the only one who could explain to me how he had become so, you know, *real*.

So I ran down the street and turned the corner. My feet did not approve of the cracked, uneven pavement and my decision to venture forth without shoes, but they would just have to put up with it.

By the time I found the Asura, he was causing quite a stir at the bus stop. The bus had actually *stopped*, which is more unusual than you would think at a bus stop, and the few people who had been on it had abandoned it because the Asura got on board. He stomped up and down the aisle, puffing smoke and snarling at the driver, who mostly sighed and looked very put-upon.

'It's way too late for this, mate,' I heard him say. 'Save the costume for the West End. Just buy a ticket so we can all go home, yeah?'

'Costume?' the Asura roared. '*COSTUME*? Do you not know who I am? I am an Asura! I am a warrior in the great Mahishasura's army! And I will help him return to this world!'

32

'Ticket,' the bus driver replied, unmoved, 'or get off.'

This couldn't possibly end well. I had to do something before someone ended up eaten or barbecued or both. I looked around desperately for inspiration, but there wasn't even a convenient stick lying around that I could hit the Asura with (not that a stick would have done much against a demon, but said stick could have at least had the courtesy to make itself available).

Then, just as I considered falling back on the noble, timeless technique of screaming very loudly, something astonishing happened.

A girl ran past me. With a sword.

She paused before she jumped on to the bus, looked back at me over her shoulder and winked. *Winked.*

Then she leapt on board and faced down the Asura. She was barely older than I was, but she was ferocious, all sharp lines and elbows and edges, the sword as much a part of her as her hands. I watched in awe as she looked the demon in the eye and didn't even tremble.

'You,' the Asura spat the word, punctuated by a puff of smoke, 'you're here. You are relentless.'

The girl smiled, but it was the least friendly smile I had ever seen. 'Did you really think I wouldn't follow you? Go back to Mysore, Asura. Go back and tell your king we won't let him return to this world.'

The Asura growled and sprang at her. The girl darted out of the way. She dragged the bleating bus driver out of his seat and pushed him out of the bus. The doors hissed shut, cutting us off from both girl and demon.

'Oi!' the bus driver shouted. 'I'll call the police, don't think I won't!'

I ignored his shouts, and the flurry of phone-camera flashes, and ran to the bus. I pressed my hands to the glass of the doors, my heart like thunder in my ears. I wanted to help, but I didn't know how.

All I could do was watch as a demon and a girl fought a battle inside a red London bus.

They moved so fast that sometimes they weren't much more than a blur. The only way I could make sense of it was by holding individual moments still, like sketches on a page. Her sword met the blade of his tail. His teeth snapped a hairsbreadth from her face. White snakes of his smoke wrapped around them. His scales gleamed too bright in the harsh lights of the bus. And the girl, somehow, held her own against the Asura. More than that, even. She was glorious. She faced him like she had been born to fight demons.

Like she had been born to fight demons.

I stared at her. At the brown skin. At the shiny dark hair cut in a sharp bob below her chin. At the brown eyes that glittered with joy and mischief I had put there. I knew that face. I knew her.

She hadn't been *born*, had she? She had come from the same place the Asura had. My sketchbook. I had *made* her.

The Asura lashed out with the jagged tail I had given him. The girl dodged and danced from seat to aisle to seat, always just out of his reach. The Asura snarled and leapt right over the seats. He swiped a powerful, clawed foreleg at her and knocked her on to the floor. I gasped as he loomed over her, his smoke darkening to crimson as he prepared to breathe fire.

I pounded my fists on the doors. 'No!' I shouted. 'Stop! Please!'

The sound made the Asura look around. It wasn't much of a distraction, but it was all the girl needed. She plunged her sword right into the dragon demon's heart.

The Asura tipped his head back and roared in pain and rage. Then he burst into smoke, which swirled in the air for a moment before it blew away.

Behind me, I heard applause. 'That was so cool,' someone said. 'How did she do that?'

The girl got to her feet and dusted herself off, then gave her audience a curtsy. Her smile was as bright as her sword.

I backed away from the doors. She opened them and hopped off the bus. 'Sorry,' she said unrepentantly to the bus driver. He glowered and stomped past her to get back to his seat.

As the bus trundled away and left the girl and me behind, I saw a plume of black smoke form in the air about halfway down the street. What now?

The girl turned to see what I was staring at. She sighed. 'Sometimes,' she said, sounding somewhat annoyed, 'their hearts aren't where they're supposed to be.'

What was that supposed to—

Oh.

As the black smoke resolved itself into the shape of the Asura, the one who just moments before had burst into that very same smoke, I realised that she hadn't killed him, after all. She'd stabbed him in the heart, but his heart had been somewhere else.

My brain could *not* cope with this.

I expected the Asura to attack us, but as soon as he took shape, he fled on four strong, clawed, scaly legs.

I briefly wondered why he hadn't used his wings and flown away, but was almost immediately distracted by the girl shouting, 'Come on! We can't let him get away!'

I had a lot of objections to this, but she was already running and I felt it would be rude not to follow.

As I chased after her, she veered abruptly into the front garden of a nearby house and came back an instant later with a bicycle. It was bright and purple, with an enormous wicker basket in front that had one forgotten potato inside.

'We're not stealing that bicycle!' I protested.

'We'll bring it back,' she said cheerfully. 'Now hurry up and get in!'

'Get in? Where—'

She leapt astride the bicycle and it suddenly became very clear where she expected me to get *in*.

'Uh, no,' I said at once. 'I am absolutely, definitely, five million per cent *not* getting into the basket.'

Fifteen seconds later, I was in the wicker basket of the bicycle and we were hurtling down the street.

My arms and legs flailed ungracefully as the girl pedalled furiously behind me, her delighted laughter in my ears. I was making noises, too, but *laughter* was not a word I would have used to describe them. The Asura was a distant speck ahead of us, but we were catching up.

'You have very nice hair, but it's quite long!' the girl yelled behind me. 'I can't see past it! You'll have to tell me which way to steer!'

'*What?*'

'YOU'LL HAVE TO TELL ME—'

'*Left!*' I shrieked as a car zipped past us, honking indignantly. 'Now right! No, wait, stay left! *Stay left!*'

We hit the crest of the hill. The next thing I knew, the girl made a sharp turn into a cobbled side street and I saw the Asura stop and turn to face us.

As soon as we hit the cobblestones, the bicycle went flying. I tumbled right out of the basket and landed with a painful *whump* on my bottom, while the girl did a backflip, landed perfectly on her feet and jumped straight at the Asura.

This time, there was no fight. As she jumped, she

wrapped both hands around her sword and raised it high. She slammed into the Asura, his bared teeth barely an inch from hers, and drove the sword down over his head and into his back, between the black-jewelled wings.

The Asura roared, a bone-rattling sound that made all the hairs on the back of my neck stand up.

But the girl didn't even flinch. She just opened her mouth and roared back.

As she yanked the sword out, the Asura burst into smoke.

'*That* should be permanent,' said the girl, satisfied.

I staggered unsteadily to my feet. My heart was beating so fast, I was pretty sure it was going to burst right out of my chest. Cars passed by on the main road and music spilt out of a window somewhere above us, but it all felt very far away.

The girl came over to where I stood, shivering in the cold. Or maybe it was the shock. We stared at each other. I tried to speak, but could only get one word out.

'Ashwini?'

Her grin grew bigger. 'So,' she said, 'you've made quite a mess, haven't you?'

4

Ashwini walked the bicycle back to its home. I hobbled after her, not quite believing any of this night had happened.

Ashwini thayi, my great-grandmother's sister. Ashwini thayi, the cautionary tale. Ashwini thayi, the family ghost. Except the *thayi* part sounded really weird now. It had been easy to say it when she was a dead ancestor like our other dead ancestors, but I couldn't bring myself to call her that now. She wasn't dead. She wasn't even old. She was barely any older than I was!

'Ashwini Kallira is supposed to be dead,' I said.

'Ashwini Kallira *is* dead.'

'But you're here.'

'Yep.'

'You have a British accent.'

'So do you.'

'And,' I heard myself say, 'you're wearing *jeans*. I'm pretty sure Indian girls didn't dress like this back when you were alive. Did jeans even exist then? How come you have jeans and a British accent?'

She stopped walking and turned back to face me. 'You plucked me out of your head,' she said, like I was being silly. 'Your head thinks in a British accent. And you drew me in jeans. You drew me exactly like this.' She swept her hands up and down to indicate her hair, her sword, her black jeans and red leather jacket. 'You look confused.'

'I *am* confused! An actual Asura just took over a bus and I'm talking to my dead ancestor's ghost. Who wouldn't be confused?'

'Let's start again. You know I'm not your actual, real ancestor, right? Like, *that* Ashwini is very dead and very not me.'

I paused. 'Um, OK, I guess I do know that, but I also feel like I don't know anything else.'

'Do you want the long explanation or the short explanation?'

'How about an explanation that doesn't sound completely bananas?'

'Ah,' said Ashwini sadly, 'you're out of luck.'

I made an exasperated noise. 'I'll take the short one, then.'

'So, you know how you came up with the idea of me and brought me to life in your sketchbook?'

'To be fair, I had no idea I was *literally* bringing you to life.'

'Well, you did. And it's what you did to everything else in that book. It's all real. Your whole world, your Kingdom of Mysore, it's all alive inside that sketchbook. Like a pocket universe tucked inside yours, I guess.'

'A pocket universe?' I said sceptically.

'I don't know, I'm thirteen,' she said. She paused to leave the bicycle in front of the house she'd borrowed it from. We walked past the bus stop (a place I would now never be able to look at the same way) and turned back on to the street where I lived. 'The point is,' she went on, 'I'm here because you drew me into that world. That Asura was here because you drew him into it, too.'

'But—'

'The Asura used a crack between the two universes to escape out of that version of Mysore and into this world. I followed him to stop him before he could hurt anyone. That's my job. I slay demons. But you know that already, don't you? That was your idea.'

'But,' I floundered again. 'But how? How could *I* possibly have turned *drawings* into real life?'

'You didn't.'

'You just said I did—'

'Let me rephrase,' she said, annoyingly cheerful. 'You made that world, but it was Mahishasura who used his powers to turn your fictional universe into a real one, hidden away inside your sketchbook.'

This completely boggled my brain but before I could reply, I heard a sound that was almost scarier than the Asura.

'Kritika Kallira, you get back in here RIGHT NOW!'

Oops. I had forgotten about Mum.

I gave Ashwini a panicked look and ran the rest of the way down the street to where Mum stood in the doorway of our house, incandescent with fury.

'It's three o'clock in the morning,' she hissed, in a quiet voice that was much, much scarier than the yelling. 'You know you're not supposed to be outside this late! What are you *doing* out here? And why are you barefoot?'

'Hiya!' said Ashwini merrily, popping up at my shoulder.

Mum's eyes narrowed. 'Do I know you? You look familiar.'

'I live three doors down,' she replied, lying so smoothly that *I* almost believed her. 'It's my fault Kiki's outside. I needed space to practice for this school play I'm in, so I came out here. Kiki saw me from her window.'

I felt a sharp elbow jab me in the ribs and, feeling horribly guilty and more than a little foolish, I quickly said, 'Yes. That.'

'Just so we're clear, Kiki,' my mother said to me, 'you looked out of your window. In the dead of night. And saw a girl with a *sword*. And your reaction was to leave the safety of your bedroom and go outside to join her?'

'Um. Yes?'

'As for you.' Mum turned to Ashwini. 'You're in a school play, in which you presumably have to use a sword in some way, and you needed space to rehearse. And your solution to this problem was to venture forth in the middle of the night and practice in the street?'

'That is correct,' Ashwini chirped, apparently oblivious to Mum's mood.

44

Mum blinked several times. 'I think you'd better go home,' she said at last. 'Kiki, back to your bedroom. Now.'

It was only when Mum said this that I remembered that the last time I had been in my bedroom, my desk, curtains and sketchbook had all been on fire.

I raced up the stairs. Behind me, Mum shut our front door and followed me. She froze in the doorway of my room.

'What happened to your desk?' she demanded.

I gawped. The flames and smoke were gone, but so were my curtains and desk. And in the spot where my desk should have been, lying on the carpet, were my slightly blackened blankets – and my sketchbook. It was exactly as I'd last seen it. Dog-eared and cracked and loved, from three months of almost constant use, but wholly unburnt.

'I,' – I couldn't think of even half an explanation – 'I don't know.'

Mum looked exasperated. 'Kiki, I have no idea what's going on, but as long as you're inside the house and not outside of it, I don't care. I'm too tired to make any sense of this right now, but we'll be having *quite* the conversation tomorrow, believe me.'

I believed her. I had never believed anything more.

'Until then, stay *put*. I love you.'

'Love you, too, Mum. I'm sorry I woke you up.'

As soon as her bedroom door clicked shut, I closed my own and whipped around to figure out what had happened. How could my desk and curtains have just disappeared? How had my sketchbook come out of the flames completely unscathed?

Yes, these questions were pretty irrelevant given everything else that had already happened, but I still required answers.

The bedroom window was open, which was probably how the smoke had cleared, but I knew I hadn't opened it. Not in October! I went over to close it and let out a startled squawk when a face appeared outside.

'Ouch,' Ashwini complained, rubbing her ear dramatically. 'Squeal right in my face, why don't you?'

'Oh, I'm so sorry,' I hissed. 'Did *I* scare *you*?'

She hopped nimbly through the window. How had she even got up here? Had she scaled the ivy?

'Ooh, cookies!' I turned around to see Ashwini seize a tin of chocolate walnut cookies I always kept by my bed. She crammed a whole one into her mouth and grinned, her teeth smeared with chocolate. 'These are good!'

'I know they are,' I grumbled. I let her take another cookie, then repossessed the tin and shoved it under my bed. 'Tell me one more time. Where did you come from?'

Mouth full, Ashwini pointed to the sketchbook.

'Mysore? *My* Mysore?'

Ashwini nodded and swallowed the last of the second cookie. 'Yep.'

'How?'

'Well,' said Ashwini, 'you know the story of Mahishasura, right? The real story?'

'I know the myth my mother told me.'

'Not a myth,' she said blithely. 'The gods, the demons, the old stories? All real. Thousands of years ago, Mahishasura persuaded Brahma to grant him a boon that would make sure no man or god could kill him. Then he gathered his Asura army and seized the Kingdom of Mysore. You know all that.'

'I also know the gods tried to get around the boon by sending a goddess to fight Mahishasura,' I said. 'Chamundeshwari.'

'She rode into battle on a lion and killed Mahishasura. The end. Yes?'

'I feel like that's a no,' I said suspiciously.

She grinned. 'Correct. It was *not* the end. Brahma's boon wasn't so easily undone. Chamundeshwari *is* a goddess, but a goddess is still a god. When she killed Mahishasura, he didn't die. Not properly. He was banished to a realm between worlds – we call it the Nowhere Place – and he's been looking for a way back to this world ever since.'

I tried to take this in. Honestly, there was a part of me that still expected someone to jump out of my wardrobe and yell, 'Gotcha!' because how could any of this actually be happening?

'Say I accept all this is true,' I said cautiously, not sure I *was* ready to accept it. 'How did my sketchbook get involved? What's so special about me?'

'Oh, don't worry,' Ashwini, an actual character from that sketchbook, replied, 'you're not special at all.'

Um. 'Ouch.'

'I don't mean that in a bad way,' she added hastily. 'I only mean this isn't *totally* your fault. You're just a kid, a little girl.'

'I'm not a little—'

'Look,' she said more seriously, 'the gods have known the whole time that Mahishasura was still out

48

there. They've been protecting every splinter between worlds, every portal. He knew he'd never get back that way, so he figured out another way. He found a path he knew no one would think to protect. Stories.'

'Stories?'

'Mahishasura's life in the Nowhere Place was sustained by the memory of people here. Every time someone thinks of him, they feed him power. That's how the gods and Asuras exist. Human memory keeps them alive. Prayers, stories, books, all of it. And Mahishasura realised that if he could claw back some of his power, he could use a fictional version of himself as a gateway, transform that fictional universe into a real one and create a new portal back into this world. One the gods wouldn't see until it was too late.'

'And you're saying that *my* Mysore is the fictional universe he picked?'

She nodded.

Suddenly, something clicked. 'The earthquake,' I said guiltily. 'That was because of me, wasn't it?'

'You started to draw him,' said Ashwini, 'and he sensed it. For you, it was an accident, but for him, it was exactly what he needed at exactly the right time. If you had stopped when the earthquake happened, he would have failed, but you didn't stop. So he used the power he's been scraping together for hundreds of years to break into your sketchbook and take over the version of him you created. To do that, he had to bring your whole world to life.'

So it wasn't totally my fault, but it was still kind of my fault. Awesome.

'You couldn't have known,' she said kindly.

'No, but that doesn't matter, does it? Whether I meant to or not, I gave him a way back into our world.'

'Not quite,' she said. 'Or rather, not yet. I said he broke *into* your sketchbook, but I didn't say he broke *out* of it. He's still there, trapped.'

There was a moment of silence. Ashwini threw a mournful look at the space under my bed. I sighed, retrieved the cookie tin, and shoved it back at her.

'Why is *he* trapped and you're not?' I asked. 'You're here. The Asura was here, too. How come Mahishasura isn't?'

'Dhashawa,' said Ashwini, her mouth full.

'What?'

She reluctantly swallowed the cookie and said, 'Dussehra.'

'The festival?'

'The boundaries of your sketchbook still have power, Kiki,' she said. 'The universe inside it is mostly closed off from every other world, including this one. Apart from one *little* tear.'

She reached for my sketchbook, which was still lying forlornly on the floor, and opened it up to my sketch of her battling the Asura. The Asura's malevolent eyes gleamed at me, and I shuddered. 'Ignore him,' Ashwini said. She pointed a little to the left of the Asura's head. 'See that?'

I looked closer. At first glance, it looked like someone had drawn a small line in bright gold ink, but then Ashwini put her hand on the line. I gasped. Instead of just resting on top of the paper, her hand sort of stretched the edges of the gold line and then, abruptly, slid *into* the page.

Ashwini pulled her hand back out. 'That's the portal, the tear between the two worlds.'

I reached out to touch it, my hand not quite steady, and couldn't believe it when my own hand vanished into the sketchbook. I wiggled it around. I could still feel it, but I couldn't see it.

'This is *so* weird!'

'It opened up today,' Ashwini told me. 'Just a tiny little crack, because of Dussehra. Millions of people were thinking about Mahishasura today since his story is part of the festival. He used up almost all of his magic when he escaped from the Nowhere Place into your version of Mysore and brought it to life, but today gave him more. *Just* enough to open up that tiny tear.'

'So why didn't he use it to get out?'

'I have no doubt he planned to,' Ashwini said with a grin, 'but I'm afraid you scuppered his plans. You drew *us* instead.' She tapped the sketchbook. 'The Asura and I were the only things you put down on *this* page, the exact page you created on the day of Dussehra, so we were the only things that could get out when the crack opened up. As long as the crack between worlds is this small, nothing from any other page can get out.'

'Can it get any bigger?'

Ashwini shrugged. 'Yes, but it'll need more magic. More than Mahishasura has right now. Remember, it took him hundreds of years of festivals, memories and stories to gather enough power to escape the Nowhere Place.'

Relieved, I said, 'So if I put the sketchbook away and never draw in it again, then he can't use me to accidentally help him any more.'

My heart hurt a little as I said it because I wasn't sure I could bear to give up this world that had kept me in one piece over these past few months, but I couldn't exactly help a monster escape, either. A picture flashed across my mind of a burning world, ashes and a few people staggering despairingly through the wreckage. It was like something out of a post-apocalyptic movie, but it also felt a little *too* possible right now. And, OK, even if it didn't get that bad, it wasn't like Mahishasura would break out and be like, 'Aha, I'm free now, I'll just go and get an ice cream!' Would he? He'd probably kill Mum and me, because we'd be the first ones he'd find, and then who knew what he'd do after that? And—

'Even if you're not helping him, he can still make the tear bigger,' Ashwini pointed out, thankfully cutting into my spiralling thoughts before they could get *really* out of hand. 'And eventually, he'll be able to use it to get free.'

'But it'll take him years to gather that kind of power. You said so yourself. Hundreds of years, maybe.'

Ashwini stared at me. 'Yes, but that's hundreds of years that *that* world will have to spend with him.'

I went quiet as I remembered everything Mahishasura did in the old stories. Children stolen from their beds, crops destroyed, starvation and fear. Monsters stalking the streets and darkening the sky. I had put all of that into my world. And now it was all real.

'What can I do?' I asked. 'I can't use a rubber on the ink, but I could rip out pages or get rid of the sketchbook? I could burn it, destroy it, *something*!'

'You saw already that fire can't destroy it,' Ashwini said. 'And even if you could rip pages out, I don't think that would erase Mahishasura from that world. But that's OK because there's something else you can do. *You* made that world, Kiki, which means you can come and go as you please. You have more power over that world than even Mahishasura does. And you can put an end to this.'

'I *draw* things! I can't stop an Asura king.'

'I'll be there to help you,' she said. 'I'll be with you every step of the way.'

Uh, what?

'You want me to go with you?' I asked incredulously. 'Go *into* my sketchbook?'

'Of course!'

'Me? The girl who can't even ride on the London Underground without worrying about the tunnels collapsing?'

Ashwini was riveted. 'Really? Are they very unstable?'

'No! They're fine, that's the point. I know it's safe, but I still spend the whole time I'm down there picturing myself crushed under rubble.'

'I'm afraid I don't see what this has to do with stopping Mahishasura.'

I felt my cheeks grow hot with embarrassment. 'It's supposed to explain why I'm the wrong person for this. I can't even make my own brain do what I want it to!'

'Maybe not, but you can do *this*,' Ashwini said firmly.

'How? What can I do to stop him that you can't?'

'It'll be easier if I show you,' she said. Then she grinned. 'I know you're scared, but I promise it won't be as hard as you think. It might even be fun.'

'You have an odd idea of what fun is.'

'Whose fault is that?' she retorted. 'You made me.'

'What about my mother? I can't just go with you to a different universe! What will she think if she wakes up and I'm not here? And there's no way she'll let me go if I ask first.'

'Oh, don't worry about that,' she said. 'I've been assured that no matter how much time you spend in the other universe, no time at all will pass here. You'll be back before she wakes up.'

'You've been assured by who?'

'Um,' she hedged. 'Well, if you must know, it was, um, Brahma.'

'*The* Brahma? Creator of all life and the world as we know it?'

'That's the one,' she said, brightening. 'When the crack between the worlds appeared and it became clear that I could use it to come here, he told me about the sketchbook and about you.'

'You mean you've actually *met*—'

'Kiki, you'll get a lot more answers if you just come with me.'

Aside from the (pretty understandable!) terror, I could feel that I was slipping once more into the familiar spiral of obsessive, inconsequential anxiety. Like, what if I went into the sketchbook and never came back and then, in thirty years, Mum opened the book for the first time and saw me in there, still eleven years old, with a speech bubble saying HELP! over my head?

I honestly couldn't believe that I had just spent my Thursday night chasing down a demon in the basket of a purple bicycle, and was probably about to jump into my own sketchbook and be eaten by a monster – and yet, somehow, the thing that my brain kept getting stuck on was the idea of my heartbroken mother discovering my whereabouts via a speech bubble.

Why was I like this?!

I yanked my thumbnail away from my mouth and reached instead for the pencil in the pocket of my pyjamas. It helped, a little.

Ashwini put her hands on my shoulders, obviously certain I was about to chicken out. 'Kiki, I wouldn't ask this of you if it wasn't important. We need you. No one else can do this.'

She still hadn't told me what *this* was.

I clenched my fist around the pencil and forced myself to take a deep, slow breath. 'OK,' I blurted, before I could talk myself out of it. 'OK, I'll go.'

'Good,' she beamed.

Then she shoved me into my sketchbook.

I didn't even have time to yelp. One minute I was about to face-plant into a book, the next I was on my hands and knees in the hot sun.

My brain stuttered to a stop there: *the hot sun*.

I had been in London, on an October night. I'd practically forgotten what the hot sun felt like.

I took slow, shaky breaths. Squeezed my eyes shut. I could feel stone under my hands, smooth stone that had been baked by the sun. A courtyard? I could hear the trickle of water close by. A fountain?

I got unsteadily to my feet. Someone was beside me.

'Kiki.' It was Ashwini's voice, electric with excitement. 'Open your eyes.'

I opened them. The light was ferocious. I blinked, dazzled, and waited for my eyes to adjust. When they did, I saw it.

My golden kingdom.

At which point, I fainted.

5

'Kiki? Kiki?'

'*This* is the girl who's supposed to save us all? Really?'

'Give her a break. She's a kid and she's had a shock.'

'I'm a kid. So are you.'

'She's not like us.'

'Clearly. Also, her clothes are ridiculous.'

'They're pyjamas. She wears them to sleep in.'

'They have rainbow unicorns all over them.'

'Go away if you're not going to be helpful. Kiki? Can you hear me?'

I opened my eyes and immediately regretted it. All I could see was vivid blue sky and impossibly bright, hot sunshine. I threw an arm over my face to shade my eyes. 'What happened?'

'You fainted,' Ashwini reminded me.

Heat rushed into my cheeks. 'Oh.'

'Don't worry,' she said kindly, helping me sit up. 'No one blames you.'

'I kind of do,' said the other voice.

I squinted at the owner. A boy, around twelve years old, with dark golden skin, brown eyes, black hair cut close to his head and an annoyed look on his face. 'What's wrong with rainbow unicorns?' I asked him.

'Don't mind him,' said Ashwini. 'That's Lej. He's rude to everyone.'

'Hi. I'm Kiki.'

'I know,' said Lej, still annoyed. It seemed a pretty safe bet that *I* was the source of his annoyance. He turned to Ashwini. 'Can we go inside now? We're exposed out here.'

As I stood up, I got my first real look at what he meant by *out here*.

We weren't in a courtyard. We were on a large balcony, with paved stone under our feet and a small, tinkling marble fountain in the very middle. Beside the fountain were my missing desk and curtains, both charred and wet. Ashwini must have pushed them out of the real world and into this one to prevent my whole house from catching fire, and Lej, I guessed, must have doused them in water while she chased after the Asura.

Once I'd had a good look at the balcony, I turned to see what was beyond it. There was a low bronze wall around the edge. And over the wall, below us, stretching all the way to the woodsy green peaks of Chamundi Hills ...

It was Mysore. *My* Mysore. I blinked, and blinked again, but it didn't disappear. The city spread out in front of me, a surreal mixture of reality and my own whimsy. The houses and shops were boxy and tidy, like the real Mysore, but I had painted them in jewel-bright colours: vibrant yellows, mint greens, deep reds, sapphire blues. A rainbow kingdom, like my rainbow unicorns. Between the colours, I could see glimpses of the streets and courtyards, each road like a winding ribbon of silver, and in the distance, at the very outskirts of the city with the paddy fields and sugar-cane farms, was the Kaveri River.

'I ...' I started to say, and then promptly forgot how to use words. 'I ...'

'Really?' Lej said to Ashwini. *'Her?'*

I barely heard him. I took a step closer to the low bronze wall. My eyes refused to blink, greedy for every detail.

Most of the city was quite low, with even the tallest houses no more than maybe three storeys tall, so the palaces towered above them. In the very heart of the city was my version of Mysore Palace, the largest and most beautiful. It had twin cream towers at each corner topped with red marble domes, enormous stone arches across the front façade, and in the centre, taller than the others, stood three golden towers with golden domes. On the peak of the middle dome was the statue of the gandaberunda, the two-headed eagle.

In the stories Mum used to tell me, the gandaberunda was the protector of the Kingdom of Mysore. In my version, the gandaberunda was a dormant stone statue that would only awaken when the city needed it most. It seemed to me that now would have been a good time for it to wake up, all things considered, but maybe the gandaberunda had other ideas.

Across the kingdom was the other palace. Lalith Mahal. In the real Mysore, it had once been a palace

62

and was now a hotel, but in this Mysore, I had made it Mahishasura's fortress. It was pure white, with open walkways and three domes, like St Paul's Cathedral in London, guarded by a hundred Asuras.

Behind the Lalith Mahal rose the Chamundi Hills, a handful of low peaks covered in deep emerald forests. I hadn't drawn in a temple at the top, like the one in the real world, because I hadn't yet got to the part of the story where the goddess Chamundeshwari had fought and won her battle with Mahishasura. I wondered where she was. I had created a version of her in my sketchbook. Her lion, too. The idea that they were somewhere in the city below, fighting their battles in the spaces between the gemstone houses and gleaming palaces, was incredible.

It was all incredible. The city was the most amazing thing I had ever seen. Every last part of it.

Well, except for maybe the castle.

I let my gaze lift up, up, *up* to the sky. To the castle suspended in the clouds. I winced. It wasn't a palace like the ones in the city. It wasn't even a proper castle with battlements and all that stuff. It was a cotton-candy castle. Pastel colours and little turrets. And it was just floating there, high above Mysore, so out of place that I would have laughed if I hadn't been only too aware that I was the one who had put it there.

On the other hand, was an adorable castle in the sky really any more impossible than everything else in front of me?

This was *all* impossible.

And yet, somehow, I was looking at it.

'You see the statue of the gandaberunda?' Ashwini's voice snapped me out of my wonder. I tore my eyes away from the city and looked at her. She rocked back and forth on the balls of her feet, excited. 'That's how you can stop Mahishasura.'

'You want me to wake the statue up? Is that even possible?'

She shook her head. 'No, only the gandaberunda decides when to wake up. No one can wake it up. Not even you.'

'Then what am I supposed to do?' I asked, confused.

'Can we have this conversation elsewhere?' Lej said, his eyes on the sky.

'I want Kiki to see first,' said Ashwini. She reached into Lej's backpack and pulled out a small collapsible telescope. She extended it, focused it and handed it to me. 'Look at the statue.'

I peered into the telescope. 'I know what it looks like,' I felt compelled to point out. 'I drew it.'

'You see the two heads of the eagle? Each with two eyes?'

'Yes.'

'What else do you notice?'

For a moment, I had no idea what she was talking about. Then, as I kept squinting into the telescope, I realised that three of the gandaberunda's four eyes were emerald green, just like I'd drawn them, but the fourth was bright gold.

'I gave the gandaberunda *four* green eyes,' I said.

Ashwini grinned. 'The golden eye is the answer, Kiki. All you have to do to stop Mahishasura is break it.'

'All I have to do is go up to the statue and break the golden eye?' I repeated dubiously. 'That's how we save this world from Mahishasura?'

'Exactly!' she said triumphantly.

'But how? And why do you need me, if all you have to do to stop him is break a statue's eye?'

Lej let out an impatient groan before Ashwini could answer. 'We have to go,' he said to her. He was still squinting at the sky.

'Just one more minute,' she insisted, and turned

back to me. 'We need you because you're the only one who can break the gandaberunda's eye, Kiki. Remember what I said about how you have more power over this world because you made it?'

'I guess that makes sense,' I said. 'But I don't get how breaking the eye will stop Mahishasura?'

'Brahma told me to think of it like an emergency exit,' she explained. 'He said that if the golden eye is broken, the magic that brought this world to life will be undone. This pocket universe and everything in it will become just ink and paper in your sketchbook again. Except for you and Mahishasura, of course,' she added. 'Neither of you came from this world, so when it becomes *un*-real again, you'll both be sent back to where you came from. So you'll go back to the real world and Mahishasura will go back to the Nowhere Place.'

'So all I have to do is break the eye and this whole thing will be over?' I asked. 'This Mysore won't be real any more?'

'Nope.'

'And you don't mind that *you* won't be real any more, either?'

Lej made a weird sound in his throat at that, but Ashwini shrugged. 'We were never supposed to be real,' she said, pretty cheerfully. 'It's right that everything should go back to the way it was.'

'As easy as that,' I said doubtfully.

She grinned. 'As easy as that.'

'OK, that's it,' Lej snapped, his patience obviously at an end. He ignored me and addressed Ashwini directly. 'Now we really *have* to go. We're standing next to the crack between worlds, with the one person Mahishasura thinks is a threat to him, so we are absolutely not safe. Frankly, I'm amazed there weren't any Asuras guarding this place when we got here, but I doubt our luck will last. *I* don't particularly care if she gets snatched by Mahishasura or one of his minions, but you seem to think she's our only hope.'

His tone told me he was by no means convinced of this. I couldn't exactly blame him, not when *I* wasn't convinced, either.

'He's right,' Ashwini said to me, with a comical grimace like she hated to admit it. 'Let's get going.'

I followed them off the balcony and into the shade of the room inside. There, I barely had a chance to take a breath or let my eyes adjust to the indoors before I was whisked away through a maze of crumbly hallways, down several flights of stairs lined with plants in terracotta pots and finally into the bright sunshine of the street outside.

For a moment, I felt the world tilt and lose focus. Right beside me, the words PRETTY CORNER MARKET were carved into a cute, rustic wooden signpost, like something straight out of an Animal Crossing game. And for some reason it was the sight of that signpost, an object I remembered sketching about a million different times before I found a style that felt just right, that made the impossible world around me suddenly feel completely and totally *real*.

Unlike the pictures in my sketchbook, this world was more than just something I could see. I could smell it, hear it, *touch* it.

Like the India I knew in the real world, there was a sense of order and rhythm in what seemed, at first glance, to be chaos. There were merchants with carts selling old books, ripe mangoes, coconuts and buttered corn scraped off the cob and wrapped up in a cone of newspaper. I could hear low voices and haggling. I could smell the butter, the mangoes, the dust.

And I remembered creating it. Creating *this* exact scene. I remembered drawing a few faces glancing anxiously up into the sky, just like the two little boys down the street were doing at that moment. I remembered drawing the lady cooking hot dosas on a skillet. I remembered sketching the lines and shadows of that old man with the cart of coconuts, expertly cracking open a hole in one of them before sticking a straw in it and taking a sip. I remembered sketching in the texture and details of the road, tightly packed cobblestones flanked by unexpectedly modern streetlights. (It wasn't like I had followed any rules. I had made this world for *me*, not for anyone else, and excellent plumbing and electricity had been essential additions to my version of an ancient magical kingdom. And considering I would need to use the bathroom sooner or later, was I now grateful for this? Yes, yes, I was.)

It was so quiet. That part was not at all like the real India. People here moved quickly, but quietly. I could hear voices, but they were soft and clipped. Like the people around me were trying to get on with their lives, sell their wares and buy their food, but also didn't want to draw attention to themselves.

Like they were scared.

Of course they were scared. Their city had been taken over by monsters.

And *I* had made those monsters.

'Come on.' Ashwini tugged gently on my arm. 'We can't stop. The moment Mahishasura finds out you're here, he's going to come after you.'

'Too late,' Lej said grimly.

Ashwini's hand tightened painfully around my wrist. I followed her gaze up, up to the rooftop of the white house we had just walked out of.

There were two silhouettes hunched over on the edge of the roof, the sun so bright behind them that it was impossible to make out anything but shapes. Horns on the head of one shadow, six bulky arms on the other.

Asuras.

I couldn't take my eyes off the shapes, my breath coming fast and shallow, but Ashwini gave me a sharp tug. 'Run,' she hissed. 'Follow Lej.'

I turned to run, and my bare feet recoiled from the hard, uneven surface of the cobbled street. Why, oh why, hadn't I stopped to put shoes on?

I heard a scream behind me and couldn't stop myself looking back over my shoulder, just in time to see the Asuras leap off the roof and land in the street, kicking up clouds of dust. People scattered, terrified.

Before I could take another step, Lej's arm shot out and stopped me. I froze as another creature, huge and fearsome, landed in front of us. We were trapped.

Curled, razor-sharp horns rose from the top of the monster's head. Even before he stepped into the sun, my whole body went cold. I knew those horns.

It was Mahishasura, the demon king.

6

I took a step back, my throat thick with fear.

Mahishasura was twice my size. Those wicked horns curled up from the sides of a buffalo's head, and he had a plate of armour over his wide, hard chest. His huge human arms and animal legs were covered in thick, bristly black fur. Two hooves thudded ominously on the cobblestones as he stepped closer. There was a sword strapped to his back. Amber eyes gleamed in a bull's face, nostrils flared, and sharp teeth flashed.

My knees felt unsteady. This was not a bad dream, or a sketch in a book, or even a minor Asura. This was the *king* of demons.

For once in my life, not a single inconsequential worry popped into my head. I wasn't thinking about the fact that the nail on my left hand's index finger was just a *bit* longer than all my other nails, or about the dirt gathering between my toes, or about how annoying the single cracked cobblestone in the otherwise unblemished street was.

I wasn't thinking about anything at all. There was no room for it; there was no room for *anything* but that monstrous face and the gleam of those long, terrible claws.

'Look at the way my people run from me,' Mahishasura said, his voice low and deep. He chuckled. 'Why do they flee? Don't they know I am a kind, benevolent king?'

'We are not your people,' Lej hissed.

Mahishasura ignored him. Those cruel amber eyes focused on me. 'Such a small girl,' he said. 'To think that you made this world, and hold the keys to my way out of it, and yet you cannot even look me in the eye without trembling.'

I tried to speak, but my mouth was dry and terror had driven words right out of my brain. I wasn't even sure I knew what words *were*.

'Of course, I should thank you, Kiki Kallira,' he went on, in that horrible, deep voice that sounded like it was always just on the cusp of a roar. 'If it wasn't for you and your desperation to escape your own mind, I wouldn't be here. I wouldn't be so very close to taking back my rightful place in the real world.'

My face burned. With just a handful of words, he had made me feel weak, cowardly and small. Because he was right, wasn't he? My art, my need to escape from my own stupid brain, *had* given him a way back.

'I know why you're here,' Mahishasura went on. His eyes flicked past me to Ashwini, whose sword was clenched in both hands and whose head kept snapping back and forth between him and the two Asuras behind us. 'I know why she fetched you from the real world. An admirable attempt to defeat me, but it was all for nothing. You must realise I cannot let you break the gandaberunda's golden eye and banish me once more?'

He bent down and, with as little effort as if he were scooping up a handful of sand, he ripped a large cobblestone out of the street. I watched as his clawed fist closed over the cobblestone and crushed it. He let the dust fall to the ground.

I gulped noisily.

'You,' Mahishasura boomed, pointing at the old man who had been selling coconuts, now trying to hide under his stall. 'Stand up.'

The old man stood up at once, his face white with terror.

'Pick up your knife,' said Mahishasura.

The old man picked up his knife.

'Now smash all of your coconuts,' said Mahishasura.

My mouth fell open. The old man's face went even whiter and his hand trembled, but he didn't dare disobey the order. He raised the knife. Down it slammed on to the first coconut, which cracked wide open and spilt sweet, whitish water all over his stall.

Ashwini's voice rose in fury. 'That's his livelihood!' she said. 'What's he supposed to live on if you make him destroy a hundred coconuts? How is he supposed to feed himself or his grandchildren?'

'You should have considered that before you brought her here,' Mahishasura growled. He flicked his eyes back to the old man. 'I said *all* of them, did I not?'

The old man bowed his head in defeat and smashed a second coconut, then a third. My eyes filled with tears. It was such an unnecessary and *mean* thing to do. I wanted to stop it, but I didn't know how.

Blinking back tears, I saw that Mahishasura was watching me, amused. 'You must see you don't stand a chance against me,' he said, his voice punctuated by the sound of coconuts cracking open.

I swallowed and forced myself to speak, even if all that came out was a croak. 'What are you planning to do with us?'

His teeth flashed in a terrible smile. 'My Asura army hasn't eaten little girl in a while.'

Before I could react to that, there was a cry behind me. I looked around to see Ashwini leap into the air with the grace of a ballerina. She soared right *over* Lej and me, her sword out and pointed right at Mahishasura's heart. In the blink of an eye, he whipped his own sword off his back and blocked her blow. Steel screeched against steel.

'Lej, take her and run!' Ashwini shouted. 'Go!'

He hesitated for just one second, but then he grabbed me by the elbow and pulled me. I let him, too shocked to do anything else. We ducked past Mahishasura, who let out a roar of fury, and we ran down the street, away from Pretty Corner Market.

I looked back once. The bright gleam of Ashwini's sword was the last thing I saw before she and the Asuras disappeared into a cloud of dust.

7

After what seemed like an eternity, Lej and I finally stopped running. I was shaking and out of breath. From the expression of disdain on Lej's face as he watched me suck in huge, noisy gulps of air, it was clear he'd seen faster and more athletic snails in his lifetime.

'I hate that we left her.' I got the words out between gulps of air. 'And the old man, too.'

Lej raised one eyebrow. 'You didn't exactly protest at the time.'

I bit my lip. Truthfully, I was woefully disappointed in myself. I had always loved stories about adventure and magic and epic showdowns between good and evil. And in spite of my fears, in spite of my anxiousness, I had always hoped that I would miraculously become brave and heroic if I were ever in a story like that.

Unfortunately, it seemed that neither pluck nor heroism came naturally to me.

'I should have tried to help her,' I said guiltily.

'How exactly would you have done that?' he asked. 'How many Asuras have you slayed in *your* world?'

'I could have done *something*.'

'You still can,' came the curt reply. 'We'll wait here for her.'

We had stopped under the shelter of an enormous banyan tree in a quiet courtyard, its limbs drooping around us like curtains. I touched the nearest leaves and remembered sketching their shape, again and again, until they looked like this.

I had *made* this tree.

I was never going to get used to this.

I sat down on the ground, back against the tree, mostly because I wasn't sure my sore feet and wobbly knees would hold me up any more. My hands were still shaking. I had put every detail of Mahishasura down on paper a hundred times over the past couple of months, yet nothing could have prepared me for seeing him stand in front of me, looming above me. A cruel king; a monster who punished the people around him just because he could.

Lej paced restlessly a few feet away. I could tell he hadn't wanted to leave Ashwini behind and that made me feel guilty all over again.

'Um,' I said. 'You know, I didn't create you.'

'And as someone who has seen the things you've created, I am eternally grateful for that.'

I must not punch him. I must not punch him. I took a deep breath. 'I guess what I mean is, I don't understand how you're here. Ashwini said this whole universe was created out of my sketchbook. So if I didn't create you, how come you exist here?'

To my surprise, Lej actually answered me. He screwed his forehead up like he was still trying to make sense of it himself, which was understandable considering he was pretty much the same age as me. 'From what we understand,' he said, 'Mahishasura used his power to transform your sketchbook into a real place. His power comes from the heavens, the same place all the gods and higher Asuras get their magic from, so it's almost an intelligent, living thing itself. To make your world real, Mahishasura's magic had to fill in the gaps.'

'Gaps?' I screwed my own forehead up. 'What kinds of gaps?'

'Like, for example, the people in the streets. They were just doodles in your sketches, but a real world is full of real people with real histories and real lives, so the magic fleshed out thousands of them. You drew Mahishasura's enormous army,' – I winced, the unspoken *thanks for that, by the way* only too clear – 'but you didn't give faces and names to all of them, so the magic did that. You created your version of your ancestor Ashwini, and made her the leader of a group of kids who spend our lives resisting your fictional version of Mahishasura, but you hadn't yet created each of us individually by the time the real Mahishasura stepped into his fictional avatar's hooves and rewrote the story.'

'So the,' – I wiggled my hands in the air to illustrate the idea of this nebulous power – 'did that too? It made you out of a doodle I put on the page?'

'That's how I exist.'

'And I guess that's why the gandaberunda has one golden eye instead of the four green ones I gave it? The magic created a way for me to collapse this world?'

'That's what Brahma told Ashwini.' He shrugged. 'The more time you spend here, the more you'll see that not everything is totally filled in. If it wasn't a necessary part of a living, breathing world, the magic didn't waste itself on it. Like, there are houses in this Mysore with incomplete stairs and no roofs. And of course, there's that.'

I followed his gaze up through the net of banyan branches to my castle in the clouds. Utterly out of reach because when I drew it, I never stopped to think, *You know, Kiki, this might be real one day so maybe you should draw a lift or a really long flight of stairs.*

'Why didn't the magic just erase that?' I asked. 'It's the definition of unnecessary.'

'It can't get rid of stuff, only add to it. This world came from your sketchbook. No god's or Asura's power can unmake what you've made.'

I considered that for a moment. Lej continued gazing up at the castle, which gave me an opportunity to look closer at him. He had a livid white scar on the back of his left hand that I hadn't noticed before, like a claw had cut him almost to the bone. A heavy stone sank deep in my stomach. Had *I* done that to him by making this world so cruel and treacherous?

'What was it like when you came to life?'

'We didn't know we came to life,' Lej said. 'It's not like we felt the moment this world became real. We

81

just *were*. For you, on the outside, this world has only existed for however long it's been since you started filling up the sketchbook. But for us, *inside* this world, we feel like it's always existed. We have memories of friends, families, our entire lives. We have history. We remember stories our grandparents told us. We remember years of trying to fight Mahishasura. We don't feel like we were once just ink on a piece of paper. We feel as real as you do.'

Just then, footsteps echoed across the dusty stone of the courtyard. I could have cried with relief when Ashwini ducked under the leaves of the banyan tree.

I jumped up and flung my arms around her. 'You're OK!'

'Of course I am.' She laughed in surprise, patting me on the back. 'You made me tough, remember?'

'What happened back there?'

'We fought,' she said merrily. 'I escaped.'

'You're *amazing*,' I said in awe.

'Did they follow you?' Lej asked.

Ashwini scoffed at that suggestion.

Inspired by how brave Ashwini had been, I was determined to be brave, too. So I said, 'Let's go and break that golden eye.'

'Um,' she said sheepishly. 'About that ...'

RIP Brave Kiki. She'd been fun for all of the fifteen seconds she'd lasted. If the look on Ashwini's face was any indication, it seemed matters were *not* going to be as easy as simply breaking the golden eye of the gandaberunda and then heading back home to my warm, comfy bed. I should have known better than to trust the merry twinkle in Ashwini's eye.

'What aren't you telling me?' I asked nervously.

'Well, for one thing, the statue will be guarded by winged Asuras,' Ashwini said. 'Now that Mahishasura knows you're here, he'll have his minions watching the gandaberunda every minute of every day. It won't be easy to get past them to break the eye.'

'Great.' I gulped.

'And,' Lej added, 'there is also the teeny, tiny problem of the maze.'

The maze?

Oh.

I had come up with it one rainy afternoon. I'd had this idea that when the old kings had been killed, Mysore Palace had rejected Mahishasura and shut him out by becoming an impassable labyrinth. A totally impossible puzzle. Trick staircases, hallways that never ended, a garden full of traps – I'd thrown them all in. Rapidly realising that no one who went past the line of columns at the entrance of the palace ever found their way back out, Mahishasura was forced to retreat from Mysore Palace and make his fortress in the smaller, less symbolic Lalith Mahal instead.

And while that part of the story had been a lot of fun to create, it was decidedly less fun now. The gandaberunda stood at the top of the tallest dome in the middle of the palace.

'We can't get to the top, can we?' I winced.

'That's kind of what we were hoping *you* could tell *us*,' Lej said grumpily. 'Considering you made it.'

'If we had wings, we could fly up to the statue.'

'We *don't* have wings.'

'Then no, I don't know how to get there,' I said. Lej looked like he was about to explode, so I added, 'It's not as simple as just knowing what to expect! I can tell you that there's a shifting maze in a botanical garden, and that there are trick staircases that lead to different places, but that doesn't mean I can figure out a maze that never stays still or find a staircase that's determined to hide!'

'You had to go and make it complicated, didn't you?'

It was a fair jab, but I couldn't help pointing out, 'I didn't know any of my silly ideas would actually matter. I would have made some very different choices if I had!'

But Ashwini, who had listened to all this in silence, was not so easily daunted. 'Well, it's worth a try anyway, don't you think?' she said. 'You may not know how to solve the palace's puzzles, but like you said, you know what to expect, so that gives us a leg up that Mahishasura never had.'

It was a good point, but I felt like someone had to state the obvious: 'What if we get stuck in there for ever?'

'Let's not,' Ashwini said brightly, and trotted off without further ado.

I looked at Lej. He looked (well, glared) at me. Then he sighed and jerked his chin in the direction Ashwini had gone, as if to say, *Go on, then*.

Reminding myself of the fact that just moments ago I had been determined to be brave, I tried (and failed) to ignore the vision my brain had conjured of my forlorn, dusty skeleton lying in the middle of the labyrinth I had created. Squaring my shoulders, I left the shelter of the banyan tree.

Ashwini and Lej knew how to get around the city without being seen, even in full daylight, so I followed them silently. The city was eerily quiet. I had made it that way, but I hadn't been prepared for how it would feel to experience it. Dust lay across cobblestones that hadn't been trod on in days, overgrown plants crept up the sides of walls, and other than a few people with carts and goods, there was almost no one out in the open. In spite of the sun's heat, I shivered.

We kept to the edges of the streets and ducked under balconies and canopies every time a shadow swooped overhead. When we got to the wide main street that led directly up to the palace there was no convenient cover, so our hiding places became more and more ridiculous: within an abandoned overturned car of the broken clockwork train, under the belly of a marble statue of an elephant, inside a bewildered farmer's cart (which was full of onions) and, worst of all, behind the cobwebby leaves of an enormous, poisonous vine.

But we made it to Mysore Palace without being gobbled up by a hungry Asura or poisoned by a vine the size of Jack's beanstalk, so at least there was that.

'Oh,' I said softly, forgetting all about the onions and cobwebs.

In spite of the unkempt grounds, the rusty gates and the neglect, the palace was breathtaking.

The gates of Mysore Palace stood open, creaky and rusty from disuse, and the grounds that bordered the palace were sad and overgrown. Mulberry bushes, ashoka trees and pepper vines lined a terracotta brick driveway that had once been used by chariots. Thorns and burrs prickled my pyjamas as we stepped between the open gates and trod carefully up the path. Ashwini kept one eye on the sky, where the monstrous shadows of demons circled high above, but I couldn't take my eyes off the palace.

It towered above us, in shades of red, cream, gold and honey. Ahead of us was a row of tall columns and enormous arches, beckoning us into the porch and deeper into the labyrinth of the palace, and above the arches were a number of red domes. In the middle, rising up out of the heart of the palace, was the biggest domed tower, trimmed in gold, at the very top of which was the gandaberunda.

We paused, necks craned to look up at the statue. Above the tallest arch, inscribed in Sanskrit around a miniature gandaberunda, was the motto of the Kingdom of Mysore:

NEVER TERRIFIED

I read those words over and over. I wanted them to make me braver.

I was so busy inside my own head that I didn't notice Lej taking a step forward until it was too late.

Between the arches and the huge front doors of the palace was a covered porch of pale terracotta tiles. There were faint patterns embossed on the tiles: lotus flowers, mandalas and diamonds. They looked like they were just for decoration, so Lej must have assumed they *were* just for decoration, and he stepped beneath the arch and on to the porch.

He didn't know that only the tiles with the lotus flowers on them were safe to step on. He didn't know because I didn't tell him in time.

'Wait!' I cried out, but his foot was already firmly planted on a tile with a diamond on it.

There was a shudder in the earth beneath us. I grabbed Lej's arm and yanked him backwards, just as the entire terracotta porch crumbled into nothing.

Lej shook himself free and stared, shocked, into the chasm that had opened up between the arches and the palace doors. There was no bottom, just yawning darkness.

'Can we get a ladder across it?' Ashwini asked, immediately trying to solve the problem. She raised a hand and squinted, like she was measuring the distance. 'No, it's too wide. What about other doors? Kiki?'

'All sealed,' I said softly, my stomach knotted up with guilt. All I'd had tow do was find my way across a palace *I* had created and break a jewel. How could I have already made such a mess of something so simple?

'*All* of them?'

'The doors at the end of the botanical garden might be open, but we can't get past the maze.' I swallowed. '*I* can't get past the maze.'

For a moment, no one spoke. Then, taking a deep breath, Ashwini made a valiant attempt at a smile and said, 'OK, I guess that's that.'

I expected Lej to be furious, but he didn't say anything. In fact, when I glanced at him, I could have sworn he looked relieved.

'We'll find another way to stop him,' he said to Ashwini.

She kept that smile on her face, but it wobbled. She had pinned all her hopes on this, on me doing this one simple thing, and I knew she didn't believe there was another way to beat Mahishasura.

'Let's go,' she said. 'The Asuras haven't spotted us yet, but let's not push our luck. Lej, you'd better go and check the others haven't got themselves into some kind of trouble. Kiki, I'll make sure you get safely back.'

'Back where?'

'London, of course. Don't you want to go home?'

I looked at her in disbelief. 'That's it?'

'What else did you expect to happen?' Lej asked. 'You're the only one who can break the eye, but apparently you can't even do that. So what's the point in you sticking around?'

I should have been thrilled and relieved. This was no place for a girl like me. I wasn't strong and brave and glorious like Ashwini.

And yet I found myself saying stubbornly, 'I'm not going. Not until I've done what I came here to do.'

'And how do you plan to do that?' Lej snapped. 'You just told us there was no other way into the palace.'

'Then I'll just have to figure something out,' I snapped back.

An enormous grin split Ashwini's face in two, bright and sincere. 'We'll find a way together,' she said, her voice bursting with new hope. 'One way or another, we'll get to that statue.'

Lej looked profoundly unconvinced.

'But first,' Ashwini added, 'breakfast!'

8

The path to breakfast involved more absurd hiding places, more thorny leaves and poisonous vines, more stinky farmers' carts (the one transporting elephant dung was a particularly low point), but eventually, we stopped.

Ashwini smiled. 'Look.'

I looked. We were in a paved square, surrounded by narrow streets and a number of tall houses of different shapes and colours. At the very heart of the square, on a perfect circle of emerald-green grass, stood a gleaming marble statue of—

I almost tripped over my own feet.

My face went so red, it felt like I was on fire. Because, well, the statue was of *me*.

Mortified, I squeezed my eyes shut, but the statue was still there when I opened them.

How could I have forgotten about the statue? It had been a quick, wistful sketch I'd dashed down in my sketchbook on a particularly bad day. It looked like me, down to my long, straight Kallira nose. And the *pose*. It was the classic superhero pose; hands on hips, feet apart, shoulders back, chest out.

I wanted to be swallowed by the paving stones beneath my feet. *Swallowed*. Immediately. For ever.

'What was I thinking?' I whimpered.

Lej let out a snorty sound that could possibly have been a laugh, but Ashwini shook her head at me. 'Don't be embarrassed, Kiki. The statue means so much to the people. Until Brahma told me about you, we had no idea who it was. Mahishasura can't destroy it, you know. He's tried. He and his Asuras can't even touch it. It's like the gandaberunda.'

'Wait,' I broke in, momentarily forgetting my mortification. 'Mahishasura really can't touch this statue? Or the one of the gandaberunda?'

'Nope.'

'Why not?'

'No one knows,' Ashwini replied. 'Maybe because the gandaberunda is the protector of Mysore? Maybe because this world came from your sketchbook? We have no idea. But whatever the reason, it makes Mahishasura absolutely spitting furious. And I, for one, call that a win.'

'That statue is who we expected you to be,' Lej said.

'It's not,' I said.

Lej raised his eyebrows as if to say, *You don't have to tell* me *that*, but Ashwini glared at him before he could say it out loud.

'Kiki,' she said earnestly, 'look at the statue. Mahishasura is a monster who takes and takes from us, but he hasn't been able to crush us. We resist him every day because we believe we can get the city we love back. And the reason we believe that, the reason we resist, is because of *you*. Because *you* made us fight. Because you created a world with monsters, but there are also thousands of extraordinary *ordinary* people in this world who resist those monsters.'

'But I'm not like you. I'm not like those people.'

'Yes, you are,' she insisted. 'Even if you don't know it yet.'

I wanted so badly to believe her, but I didn't know if I could. How could the girl who lay awake in the dark worrying about murderous geese and unlocked front doors be the same as the one on the marble plinth? The statue was just an echo of a Kiki who was gone now. My own brain had made me someone else and the new me wasn't the girl this world needed me to be.

But what if I could be? What if there was a chance Ashwini was right? After all, hadn't I created that statue because it was a version of myself I wanted to be? What if I could be one of those extraordinary ordinary people who resists instead of running?

I clenched my hands inside the pockets of my pyjamas. One of them curled around my pencil and it made me feel a little better. Braver. A bit more like the marble girl; the plucky heroine of her own story.

I had absolutely no idea if I could save Mysore from Mahishasura, but I would try. With all of my messy, anxious heart, I would try.

Now that I'd recovered somewhat from the sight of the statue, I remembered the *other* thing it meant. 'If we're in this square,' I started, 'then that means—'

'Yep.' Ashwini beamed. 'That means we're home.'

With that, she gestured for me to go ahead. It was the first time either of them had let me lead the way, and I didn't need telling twice. I knew exactly where to go.

I crossed the square to a weird, crooked, tall, pale-blue house with a ruby-red door. It looked like someone had picked three different types of houses and stacked them on top of each other, without the slightest interest in whether any of the edges lined up. And by someone, I meant me. Oops.

Beside the bright-red door, on a little wooden plaque, were the words CROW HOUSE.

To an Asura, the house would look the same, except there would never be any lights in the windows, never any noises from inside, never any sign that anyone lived here. The house had a mind of its own and it was determined to hide the mismatched family of Crows who lived inside.

I knocked tentatively on the door. It opened immediately, as if someone had been on the other side, waiting.

But there was no one on the other side. The *house* had opened the door.

When I looked down the bright hallway, filled with

rain boots, jackets and one very sharp arrow, I saw a face appear at the other end.

'It's you!' a little voice whispered in awe.

Lej sighed and went in first. I followed him in, and Ashwini came after me and shut the door firmly behind us.

'Behold,' she said grandly, 'our headquarters!'

Crow House was a whirlwind of sunny windows, loud noises and an immediate onslaught of excited faces and loud questions. It felt like there were at least a hundred of them, but it turned out to only be four.

'Oi!' Lej barked. 'Pipe down!'

It gave me some comfort to know he used that tone on everyone, not just me, but it had absolutely no effect on the horde. They just giggled at him, before going straight back to crowding around me and chattering at the tops of their voices.

Ashwini put her hand to her mouth and let out a piercing whistle. The house went silent immediately.

'Is that any way to greet our guest?' she asked, mouth twitching as she tried and failed to suppress a grin. 'Kiki's going to think you were all raised by jackals!'

'Not jackals,' said a cheeky male voice. 'Just crows.'

'Put a sock in it,' Ashwini said in the exasperated tone I'd often heard Emily use on her little sister. 'Give Kiki some space and a chance to take a breath.'

They vanished in a clatter of footsteps and wheels.

I raised my eyebrows at Ashwini, who shrugged and said, 'I'm *very* good at keeping them in line. Lej, on the other hand,' she added, rather smugly, 'is not.'

Lej's only response was to roll his eyes. Ashwini gave him an affectionate elbow in the ribs as she lowered her sword to the floor and shrugged out of her leather jacket. I looked around, one hand touching the pale, sunshine-yellow paint of the hallway wall. I was torn between curiosity about the kids I'd just seen and terror at the prospect of living up to their expectations of me.

I was lost in my own thoughts when I heard Ashwini say, 'Let's go sit down. You must be exhausted!'

I opened my mouth to say that I was indeed exhausted, not to mention starving, but instead I found myself too fascinated to resist asking, 'Actually, is it OK if I see the rest of the house first?'

She beamed. 'Of course! Come on, I'll show you around and you can meet the Crows properly.'

The first room she showed me was the front room, just off the hallway, and it was obviously their living room. It was an explosion of toys, books and plump, faded cushions. The walls were panelled in warm-coloured wood and lined with shelves and sketches, and there were two mismatched sofas and one squashy armchair on top of a shaggy rug. The big bright window across the room looked out on to the square and statue.

It was bizarre, seeing the room I remembered putting down on paper – including my sketches on the walls! – now filled with the personal possessions of people I didn't know. Someone's rumpled striped sweater tucked into a corner of a sofa, someone else's half-drank mug of hot chocolate, a pile of books and a notebook with neat handwriting, a doll, a peculiar cactus, someone's reading glasses, a role-playing board game called *Giants & Gargoyles*. Whole lives were on display in this room, *real* lives, and it made my head spin.

'This is where we all hang out,' Ashwini explained a little unnecessarily. 'So the room kind of looks like all of us.'

A second door across the hallway from the front room branched off to the kitchen, which Ashwini bypassed for the moment, and we went down the hall, past a crooked, narrow flight of stairs, to a third door at the end. It was open, but Ashwini gave it a courteous tap anyway before standing back to nudge me in ahead of her.

The presence of a cosy, neatly made bed pushed against the wall told me this was a bedroom, but otherwise I would have been sure I'd walked into a tailor's shop. Scissors, pins, a glue gun, bolts of fabric and a rusty old sewing machine cluttered the surfaces of two tables on either side of the room, and there were scraps of a dozen different kinds of materials – was that *chainmail*? – all over the floor. Mannequins made out of twisted pieces of wire were dotted around what little space was left, each draped with some kind of half-finished item of clothing.

There was a boy in a wheelchair at one of the tables. He looked like he was about Ashwini's age, and he had dark brown skin, curly black hair, faded blue jeans and a grey T-shirt, and socks with tiny elephants all over them. He gave me a quick, shy grin when he saw me in the doorway.

'This is Jojo,' said Ashwini.

'Hi,' I said, and went on in awe, 'this is amazing. Did you make all this yourself?'

'Jojo makes our costumes,' Ashwini explained as Jojo nodded, gratified by my reaction. 'He also patches up all our clothes, which is handy considering new clothes are hard to come by.'

'I'm *also* the Crows' archer,' Jojo added, gesturing to a bow propped up against the wall.

'Hang on,' I said. 'Costumes?'

'You know, the clothes we wear when we fight Asuras? Our colours?'

'Black with red and gold,' I said, suddenly remembering the superhero-style battle-gear ideas I had doodled in my sketchbook months ago.

'That's it,' said Jojo. 'I'm working on yours right now.'

My smile faltered. The memory of Mysore Palace and my total failure came rushing back. 'That's really nice of you, but I don't think I've done anything to earn a costume of my own.'

Jojo's brow furrowed in confusion, but Ashwini quickly intervened. 'You brats haven't eaten already, have you?'

'As if Suki would have let us wait for you,' he scoffed. 'You know she's a bottomless pit. Not that any of us would say no to a second breakfast ...'

Ashwini rolled her eyes and led me out of the room.

I followed her up the crooked stairs to the second floor, where more doors branched off a sunny corridor lined with plants in clay pots.

The first door led to a bedroom that I knew at once had to be Ashwini's: the simple wooden walls were lined with no fewer than four swords, seven knives, two tridents, one spear and one unexpected baseball bat. The floor had wooden floorboards, all scuffed and worn down from what I could only assume was Ashwini practicing with the aforementioned weapons; and the few clothes I could see were in messy piles on the unmade bed and armchair.

'I'm the warrior.' Ashwini shrugged by way of explanation. 'If you think this is weird, wait till you see Lej's room.'

She beckoned me across the corridor to a room that immediately hurt my eyes.

Lej wasn't in his room, which was probably just as well because I wasn't sure he would fit. Every available surface of the room was crammed with objects of every possible kind. I could see bottles of fizzy liquid, rusty weapons, broken clocks with their mechanics laid out, incomplete pieces of armour, a box of cake mix, something that looked like a microwave, wrenches and screwdrivers and other tools, a grubby porcelain doll, torn and stained maps, cutlery, a lamp without a lampshade, a lampshade without a lamp, a chipped marble bust, dishcloths and much, much more.

My brain felt intensely, violently itchy at the sight of it. I wasn't especially tidy, and it wasn't like I enjoyed cleaning or anything, but my brain needed some kind of order to feel calm. Even if something was messy, if it made sense to me, it was fine. But Lej's room was chaos, and this kind of chaos, to me, was kind of like having an itch in your armpit in the middle of a school play. No matter how bad it gets, you can't scratch it.

'I ...' I tried and failed to think of something to say.

Ashwini laughed at my reaction. 'Lej is more of a magpie than a Crow,' she said. 'But this isn't just for show. All this stuff? Lej will find a way to make it useful. When we need weapons, Lej finds them. When Jojo needs fabric or material, Lej gets it. Whatever we need, he gets it, whatever it takes. Most of this stuff may or may not be stolen,' she added primly.

I turned back to the room in fascination, and, now that I knew to look for it, I saw the pattern my brain so badly needed. Every object in the room had its place, and its purpose, and it would help the Crows fight the monsters. The bulb in that lamp without a lampshade could be used to make a flashlight, that chipped marble bust could be traded for food and the porcelain doll—

'Why the doll?' I asked, trying and failing to think of a way a doll could be used to defeat Mahishasura.

'Oh, that,' said Ashwini. 'Suki loves dolls. I expect Lej will give it to her once he's cleaned it up.'

Such a small, kind gesture seemed so completely unlike the Lej I had met that I gaped at her for a moment.

'Come on,' she said. 'The twins are at the end of the hall.'

The last room on the second floor was the biggest of the three by far, which made sense because it was clear two people lived in it. There were identical twin beds in the room, one made and the other unmade, and there were identical twin girls, but other than that, the two halves of the room were so different it was almost comical.

One half was lined with bookshelves, each crammed with creased, cracked, old and dusty books. There were neat piles of books on the bed, on the round yellow carpet, on the cool marble floor. There were books lying open, books with scribbles and sticky tags, notebooks, empty books, books so full of papers they were tied shut with ribbon. Titles like *The (True) Illustrated Book of Indian Folklore* and *How to Beat a Big Bad Wolf* winked up at me in the sunlight.

The other half of the room looked like someone had transplanted an entire garden indoors. The relatively small space was filled with big potted plants, packets of seeds, window boxes of herbs and succulents, glass terrariums filled with flowers and a trellis covered with brightly flowered vines. Between the lush greens of the plants were even more unexpected objects: a microscope, an apothecary's kit of bottles and beakers and a small electric cauldron that appeared to be brewing something thick, gold and bubbly.

The twins themselves were about ten years old, with brown skin, dark braids like Dorothy in *The Wizard of Oz*, and round cheeks that dimpled as they smiled. One of them stayed curled up on her neatly made bed, with her books, but the other beamed and bounded out of her indoor garden.

'I'm Suki,' she chirped, 'and this is my sister, Samara.'

'Hi,' said Samara shyly, and I recognised hers as the little voice I'd heard at the door saying, 'It's you!' in such awe.

'Hi,' I said, possibly even more shyly. 'It's nice to meet you both.'

'We've been *dying* to meet you!' the less shy twin, Suki, said. 'You're the coolest person *ever*. You made this *whole* world!'

'Well, I—'

'And,' she continued, giddy with excitement, 'you're here to get rid of Mahishasura once and for *all*, so that's obviously an *awesome* bonus!'

'Well, I—'

'Suki,' Ashwini warned, exasperated, 'remember what we said about not piling on the pressure? Kiki's still getting her head around all this.'

'I also haven't had much sleep,' I added hastily. 'It's not you, honestly, it's me. *Everything* feels like too much right now.'

Suki patted me on the shoulder. 'Not to worry,' she said cheerfully. 'You'll feel a lot better after breakfast. I know I always do.'

Ashwini, who had approached the mysterious

106

bubbling cauldron, now said, 'This is coming along, isn't it? Nice work, brat.'

I peered at the frothing golden liquid inside the cauldron and, without thinking, stuck my finger out to touch it.

'*Eeeek!*' Suki shrieked, diving in front of me. 'No! Absolutely *no* touching!'

'It's poisonous,' said Samara, from her side of the room.

'Oh,' I squeaked.

'Suki's our apothecary,' Ashwini told me, gently but firmly nudging me away from the cauldron. It was probably for the best. I clearly couldn't be trusted. 'If you need a potion or a poison, she's your girl. That's what all the plants and flowers are for.'

'That, and they're lovely to look at,' Suki added, sighing happily as she looked around her small, bright, green space.

'I can't believe you think *I'm* cool,' I said, amazed. '*This* is cool.'

Suki's face glowed with pride. She took my arm and tugged me over to her sister's side of the room. 'This is where Samara does all her research,' she said. 'She loves books. Like, *loves* them. If you ask me, it's not as fun as what *I* do, but I guess someone someday might need to know what a wolf Asura's greatest weakness is.'

'Says the girl who always smells like wet dirt,' her twin replied with a grin. 'I'll take my books over your plants, thanks.'

'I do *not* always smell like—'

'Ooookay,' Ashwini said quickly, looking up at the ceiling like she was asking the universe how she ended up in this situation. 'Kiki and I are going to go and see the rest of the house.'

'And then breakfast?' Suki asked hopefully.

'You already had breakfast!'

'But I'm *starving*.'

Ashwini groaned and pinched the bridge of her nose. 'If the Asuras don't murder them,' she said to me, 'I will.'

9

There were just two doors at the top of the next flight of crooked stairs. One was closed, but the other had been flung wide open. As Ashwini and I stepped on to the landing, there was a *whoop* of glee from beyond the open door. Then a *boom* rattled the entire house.

I looked at Ashwini in alarm, but she was unfazed. 'That happens at least twice a day,' she said breezily. 'You'll get used to it.'

A young boy with sticky-uppy black hair and twinkling brown eyes stuck his head out of the room at the sound of her voice, and his whole face lit up when he saw me.

I sucked in a breath. I knew that face. 'Pip?'

'You know Pip, of course,' Ashwini said, and Pip grinned at me.

I did know Pip. Other than Ashwini, he was the only one of the Crows I had got around to putting down in more detail in my sketchbook. But the truth was, I had created Pip long before I had created Ashwini, the Crows, Crow House, or even my Mysore.

He had been my very first friend; a twinkly, merry boy I had conjured up when I was about four or five. I had still been brave sunshiny Kiki back then, so Pip had been my companion on endless adventures: we were pirates, superheroes, princesses. In fact, Pip had been so real to me that I would make Mum set an extra plate for him at the table ('Salt is his favourite meal,' I would inform her, insisting that the salt shaker always be within his reach), and I would tell other people with perfect seriousness that I had a brother (Mum usually had some very awkward questions to answer when I did that).

The flood of happy memories made it difficult, suddenly, to breathe. I had seen a lot of amazing, terrifying and impossible things since a monster had materialised in my bedroom, but none of them had got to me quite like meeting Pip did now. The sight of him, this impossible echo of a happier, sunnier time and a happier, sunnier me, made tears prickle my eyes.

'Kiki!' His mischievous face lit up like he had just found a long-lost friend. 'I'm so happy to see you again! Come look at this. You'll love it!'

His easy familiarity made my heart hurt. 'You *remember* me?'

He scrunched up his forehead. 'Well, I think so,' he said. 'I remember most of my life here in Mysore, but I also have these other memories of a little girl with a big grin, a pirate ship and a *lot* of salt. I used to think they were just dreams,' he added, 'but then Ashwini told us what Brahma told her, and I realised it had to be you. *You* were the little girl.'

I almost burst into tears right then and there, but Pip grabbed me by the hand and whisked me into his room, which was absolutely *bonkers*.

There was an actual carousel in the middle of the room, for a start, and a tree growing on the *inside* of one wall, stretching all the way up through the ceiling to the sky. A tiny tree house nestled in the higher branches of the tree, just like the tree house I used to pretend Pip and I were in every time we draped a sheet over a table and hid underneath. And scattered around the room were bits of our shared childhood: a stuffed rabbit I had lost years ago, the crown we fought over when we couldn't decide who got to be the princess and who got to be the knight, the flag we tore off a rival pirate's ship during one of our adventures. Every adventure I pretended to have with my imaginary friend, every story we told each other, every toy we loved – it was all here.

'I don't know what to say,' I said, my voice all choked up. 'I ... This is ...'

'Here.' Pip grinned, handing the stuffed rabbit to me. 'I believe this is yours.'

'Petey!'

'Uh, I *think* you mean Hairy Hare-Hare,' Pip corrected me, eyes twinkling wickedly.

I gasped, affronted. 'That was a terrible name six years ago, and it's a terrible name now. This is Petey.'

And then I realised how weird and ridiculous this whole situation was, and both Pip and I burst out laughing while Ashwini shook her head in bemusement. 'It looks like you've both found the missing halves of your souls,' she said wryly.

'What was that explosion a minute ago?' I asked Pip.

His grin grew even bigger, which I hadn't believed was possible. 'Stink bomb,' he said gleefully. I blinked.

'You can't smell it because I haven't yet added the stinky part, but I promise it'll be *awful* when I do.'

Ashwini grimaced slightly as she said, 'Pip is the one who creates the handy distractions we need when we're in a sticky spot.'

'That's just a boring way of saying I'm the captain of fun and tomfoolery,' said Pip.

Ashwini rolled her eyes for the millionth time since I'd met her, but her mouth twitched like she was trying not to smile. 'I seem to remember we've talked about your use of the word *captain* and the authority it inaccurately implies.'

I giggled.

'Well, I think that pretty much covers the tour,' Ashwini said to me. 'Let's go to the kitchen.'

Pip whooped. 'Second breakfast!'

'I hate you all,' said Ashwini.

Back on the ground floor, the kitchen was small and spotless; a bright room painted in peach. It was starkly, unnervingly familiar. I remembered spending *ages* sketching in the smallest details of that rack of spices, determined to name every single one. I remembered drawing the ice tray inside the fridge and the blue door in the corner. I remembered browsing through a gazillion reference photos of dining tables before deciding on the rustic wooden one now stretched across most of the empty floor space. I even remembered drawing the little chip in the table from where Pip tripped one time and almost knocked out a tooth.

The others had already gathered at the table by the time Ashwini, Pip and I went in. Lej raised his eyebrows. 'Is she going to be eating *our* food?'

'What else is she supposed to eat?' Ashwini demanded.

'One of those rainbow unicorns on her pyjamas? A piece of that ridiculous castle in the sky?'

'Shut it,' said Ashwini, and pointed to an empty chair at the table. 'Why don't you sit down while I get breakfast sorted out, Kiki? I'll show you where you can sleep after we've eaten.'

I sat down obediently. 'Do you live here all by yourselves?' I asked, before I could think better of it. 'Where are the grown-ups?'

There was a split second of silence before Lej said, 'You didn't give us any.'

I opened my mouth, but couldn't speak. *You didn't give us any.* I could hear the bitterness and resentment in his voice and, frankly, I couldn't blame him. Because I didn't give them any grown-ups, did I? I had specifically created a group of rebel *kids*.

'We do live here by ourselves,' Ashwini told me. 'But there's an old lady next door who pays us to do odd jobs for her and there are a couple of people at the market who help Lej find weapons and other gear, so it's not like we're completely alone.'

'Grown-ups are no fun, anyway,' Pip piped up.

Lej didn't reply, but his hard eyes met mine for a moment and I could guess what he didn't say. That he'd have liked to have an adult around to actually look after them. That he didn't want the only person he could rely on to be Ashwini, who was also a child.

'I never planned for any of you to actually *live* the life I put down in my sketchbook,' I said. 'I'd have done it differently if I had known. I'm so sorry.'

'No more of that,' Ashwini said. 'You came here to help us, Kiki. There's nothing to be sorry for. Lej,' she went on, 'I think you can help me with breakfast today. Maybe it'll keep you quiet for more than thirty seconds.'

As soon as Ashwini and Lej fired up the stove, I was swallowed up by a tsunami of questions.

'Are you going to kill Mahishasura with a sword or a spear?'

'Do you usually wear your pyjamas in the daytime?'

'Who's going to rule Mysore once you've got rid of Mahishasura? Can it be me?'

'Couldn't you have given us cool outlaw names? Lej calls me "Suki, the Bitey Mongoose" and I don't think that sounds very impressive.'

By the time Ashwini announced that breakfast was ready, I was exhausted and very grateful for the silence that fell immediately over the kitchen as everyone crammed their mouths full.

Ashwini triumphantly plopped a plate down in front of me. 'And lo,' she said, 'a perfect South Indian dosa!'

It had been so long since I'd had a proper dosa that my entire body perked up at the smell. I took a cautious bite. The crisp brown edges crunched in my mouth before the soft white buttered middle melted in.

My eyes widened. 'This is amazing!'

Ashwini beamed. 'Come over here and you can make the next one. I'll show you how.'

I spent the next half hour at the stove, trying to copy her. The familiar rhythm of cooking was soothing, as I measured ingredients and listened to the sizzle of batter, exactly like I did when Mum made pancakes at home, and for a few minutes, my brain was quiet and Mahishasura seemed very far away.

When I yawned for the third time, Ashwini cut the dosa lesson short. She showed me to a bathroom, where I felt enormous gratitude, once again, for my decision to include running water and toilets that flush in my made-up world. I peeled off my rainbow pyjamas, rinsed dirt off of my bruised, sore feet and soaked in a hot bath for a few minutes. Suki had offered me a T-shirt and shorts, so I put them on once I was clean and went back out to find Ashwini.

She led me back up to the top floor, to the closed door across the corridor from Pip's room. 'Whose room is this?' I asked curiously.

She looked amused. 'Yours, of course.'

'I have a *room* here?'

'The house must have known you'd be coming,' she said, and pushed the door open.

It was a pretty room, with pale yellow walls and a soft, carpeted floor and a big window that looked out over the city's skyline. The room didn't have much of the hectic chaos and personality of the others' rooms, but it had the kind of furniture I'd always dreamt about: a huge fluffy four-poster bed; white shelves with plants, books and canvases; a sliding ladder for the shelves; a polished desk with a comfy chair; and several trays and boxes of art supplies.

It was bright and sunny and *orderly*. It made my brain ridiculously happy.

'Thanks, Crow House,' I whispered.

Ashwini smiled. 'One of the best things you did was give us this house, Kiki. It can't cook us dinner or replace our worn-out shoes or help us fight the monsters, but it keeps us safe and it gives us everything we need to make it feel like home.'

'But if we win,' I said, 'if we break the gandaberunda's eye and banish Mahishasura, this house will be gone, too. It'll just be a picture in my sketchbook.'

'It's a small price to pay for saving the world,' she said gently, and left.

As the door clicked shut behind her, I limped over to the fluffy bed. I wanted to look out of the window, to see more of this city, *my* city, but I was too tired.

I crawled under the cool, soft covers and, for the first time in months, fell asleep instantly.

And, after what felt like only minutes, I woke to the earth-trembling roar of a lion.

10

Still reeling from the roar, I let out a startled yelp when Lej stomped his way into my room without so much as a knock. 'Your presence is required downstairs,' he said.

I was sure there were people in the world who, upon hearing the roar of a lion, felt like the most sensible course of action was to make their way towards the sound. Me, not so much.

'I'm good here, thanks,' I said.

'You truly are the hero Mysore needs,' Lej replied with an obnoxious amount of sarcasm. 'Come on. The lion's on our side, I think.'

'You *think*?'

'He asked for a cup of tea and didn't eat any of us, so yeah, I am assuming he is on our side.'

I goggled at him for a full minute before deciding I didn't have the energy to figure out whether he was joking. I clambered reluctantly out of bed and followed him downstairs.

The kids were all crowded around the door to the front room, which had been shut fast, their ears literally pressed to the door. Jojo even had his chair wheeled close and a glass wedged between his ear and the wall.

'Kiki, there you are!' Suki's attempt at a whisper was practically a shout. 'Try to speak as loudly as you can when you're in there, OK? We want to hear everything!'

Wait, I was supposed to go in there and face the lion *alone*?

Before I could protest this absurdly unfair turn of events, Lej opened the door and pushed me into the front room.

I had seen the front room earlier, so it was impossible not to notice the very significant difference between then and now: there was an enormous lion stretched out by the window, with a cup of tea in front of him.

And then Ashwini said, 'Here she is,' and I turned my head to look at who she was talking to.

Suddenly, the lion seemed like the least alarming thing in the room.

Because the other visitors were gods.

'Kiki, this is Chamundeshwari,' said Ashwini, somewhat unnecessarily. I had known her the instant I saw her: she was my version of the warrior goddess, down to her armoured tunic, a sword twice the size of the one Ashwini had carried around last night, and the gold glitter sprinkled across her black braid and dark brown skin. (I liked glitter. Seeing her now, though, it occurred to me that she probably liked having it *on* her a lot less.)

Which meant the enormous tea-drinking creature by the window was Chamundeshwari's lion. The one she rode into battle.

I gave them both a weak smile.

'And this,' Ashwini went on, clearing her throat, 'is Vishnu.'

I gulped. 'Um.'

'That is not a real word in any dialect,' Vishnu, a literal god, replied sternly.

He looked like any other man, except for the golden crown on his close-cropped head of dark hair, but the air around him seemed to crackle with electricity.

121

He had dark, piercing eyes that looked decidedly unimpressed by what was in front of him.

Which is to say, me.

'You need not bow,' he said generously, which made me immediately worry that I should have. I already knew this was going to torment me later. I would obsess over every second of this conversation, wondering if an actual god now thought I was a complete twit.

Vishnu looked at Ashwini and Lej. 'We would like to speak to Kritika alone.'

It wasn't a request, so I wasn't surprised when Lej ducked out of the room immediately. Ashwini didn't look happy. She hesitated, which I appreciated, but Vishnu gave her a severe look. Biting her lip, she left.

Alone with two gods and a lion, I, of course, ramped up my worrying. I didn't actually know how to stand in the presence of such lofty heavenly figures. I kept my back perfectly straight, but after a lifetime of huddling, with the worst posture possible, over sketchbooks and paper, it was surprisingly uncomfortable. Was slouching acceptable? Would they smite me if I sat down? What was I supposed to say?

Luckily, Vishnu seemed to feel no contribution from me was necessary. 'I am here from our world on behalf of the other gods, Kritika,' he said.

It's Kiki, I wanted to say, but didn't dare. *Kritika* chafed at my brain, but *Kiki* had a certain symmetry.

'When Mahishasura entered *this* universe,' Vishnu went on, 'we gods sensed his power at work and realised he had found a way back to our world. The tear between this world and ours is still small, fortunately, but given time, we have no doubt Mahishasura will find a way to rip it wide open and escape. It is imperative that he is not permitted to do that.'

I nodded. 'I know that.'

'I am glad to hear it. Then you are prepared to defeat him?'

'Well, if by *defeat*, you mean break the—'

'By *defeat*, I mean defeat,' he said firmly. 'He must be defeated permanently. That means he must be destroyed.'

I blinked. 'Kill him? You think *I* can kill an Asura? *That* Asura?' This was absolutely *not* what I had agreed to. I turned to Chamundeshwari, who hadn't yet said a word. 'Can't you do it?'

'Lord Vishnu says that the version of me in the real

world already tried,' she replied. She had a warm, musical voice. 'She was only able to banish him, which is why he's here now. So I am afraid I could do no better.'

'No man or god can kill Mahishasura,' Vishnu reminded me. 'Brahma's boon still protects him. It cannot be revoked. We tried to subvert it once, and we failed. Chamundeshwari is a goddess who was made by gods, and thus could not truly defeat Mahishasura. We cannot repeat that mistake. You, on the other hand, are neither a man nor a god.'

'No, I'm a girl, but—'

'Yes, regrettably.'

That made me pause. *Regrettably?*

'Little girls are not very strong or powerful,' he said calmly, 'and you are, unquestionably, a little girl. But that potentially also makes you the only one who can get past Brahma's boon.'

'There are other girls here,' I pointed out. 'Ashwini, for one. She would be a much better choice.'

'And if you think the right thing to do is to send her after Mahishasura, feel free to do so,' said Vishnu. 'I, however, think that this world was *your* creation and it is therefore *your* responsibility to ensure its evils do not find their way back to our universe. In any case,' he added, 'your friends outside this room *have* been trying to destroy Mahishasura. They have failed. You, however, have not yet tried.'

'But—'

He raised a hand to cut me off. 'I assure you, I am sympathetic to how impossible this task must seem,' he said. 'You are just a child, a girl who is more comfortable with her pencil than with a sword, and you do not have the typical qualities of a hero. But you are also the only line of defence we have between Mahishasura and the world on the other side of that tear, so you'll have to do.'

I stood in stunned silence, my cheeks hot and red. Even Lej, I was pretty sure, had more faith in me than *this*.

OK, maybe not.

'But,' I tried again, 'I don't even know how to use a sword.'

'Then learn,' Vishnu replied.

'But it makes far more sense for me to break the—'

'Stop,' he said impatiently. He didn't raise his voice, but his tone made me go quiet immediately. 'We do not have time to waste on cowardice. I trust you will do what is necessary. Now I must return to my place in the heavens. Chamundeshwari will do her best to rally the people of Mysore to assist you and your friends in the battle that is to come.'

'That's it?' I said in disbelief. 'You're a *god*. Why won't you stay and help?'

He looked sternly down at me. 'Do you think there is no other crisis in the universe that needs my attention? There are a thousand problems I cannot solve if I stay here to hold the hand of an anxious little girl.' I flinched, and he went on, 'In any case, the best way I can help, as you put it, is by protecting the other side of the tear so that nothing else is able to escape into our world.'

Somehow, I found the nerve to say, 'And who cares what happens to *this* world as long as *ours* is safe, right?'

'That is up to you, is it not?' said Vishnu. 'If you stop Mahishasura, both worlds will be safe from him. If you fail, both worlds will suffer.'

And so would the people in those worlds. Like my mother. If the tear got any bigger and monsters started to break out of my sketchbook, she would be the first one they'd find.

'I get it,' I said quickly. I couldn't bear to think about

them getting to Mum. All those times I'd worried about something terrible happening to her? All those times I thought I'd forgotten to lock a door or close a window and had been convinced she'd been murdered? That's what had done this. All that time I'd spent worrying about losing her had jinxed her, I was sure of it, and now she really *was* in peril.

'Good,' said Vishnu. 'Then you know what you must do.'

'It is a great burden to place upon one child,' Chamundeshwari interjected, with what may have been pity. 'And it will put her life at grave risk.'

Vishnu was unmoved. 'She is the architect of this world. There is nothing I can do about that.'

Unexpectedly, the lion raised his beautiful, terrifying maned head from where he had been lapping at his tea. 'I will stay with her.'

I squeaked in shock. 'You can speak?!'

His great jaws opened and a deep voice rumbled out of his mouth. 'Obviously.'

'His name is Simha,' Chamundeshwari offered.

I frowned. 'That's just *lion* in Kannada.'

'Yes,' said the lion, 'it is. And it is my name because *someone* didn't give me a better one.'

Oh.

Awkward.

'I will stay and offer her some measure of protection,' Simha said to Vishnu.

'As will I,' Chamundeshwari added. 'I have much to do in the city, but I will check in on her.'

Vishnu shrugged his armoured shoulders. 'Very well. Then with that, I will bid you all farewell. Good luck to you, Kritika Kallira. I suspect you will need it.'

11

'Did you tell him about the gandaberunda?'

It was the first thing Ashwini wanted to know. She and I were alone in the kitchen, under the pretext of fetching snacks for everyone.

I shook my head. 'No, he didn't want to listen to anything I had to say.'

She was silent for a moment, so I told her what Vishnu had said. She looked uneasy. 'He really said you had to kill Mahishasura? Kiki, in the nicest possible way, you're not exactly ...'

'I know, it's ridiculous,' I said emphatically. 'There's absolutely *no* way that I can fight him and win. Much as I'd love to be you, I'm very, very much not.'

Ashwini's smile was slightly crooked. 'You don't want to be me.'

'You're everything I wish I was.'

Her brow furrowed and she considered me in silence.

'Vishnu must have known about the gandaberunda anyway,' I went on. 'If Brahma told you about the statue, the other gods probably know about it, too.'

'And yet he thinks you should fight Mahishasura,' said Ashwini.

'Apparently,' I said, gnawing on my thumbnail.

The kettle whistled. Ashwini took it off the stove and poured hot water into cups. I spooned in chocolate powder and added some milk to each cup.

'I get that destroying Mahishasura will get rid of him for good,' Ashwini said. 'That's probably why it's the more attractive option for Vishnu, but it's not realistic. Trying to fight him will get you killed. Breaking the gandaberunda's eye, on the other hand, will save both our worlds for a hundred years.'

'So we stick to Plan A?' I asked.

'I think that would be best.'

I couldn't pretend I wasn't relieved that all I had to do was break a statue's eye (you know, once we figured out how to get past a mistrustful palace), but even that seemed like such an enormous thing to someone whose biggest adventure until today had been the time I fell into a pond and swallowed a bug.

What if I couldn't do it? What then? I thought about Mum, asleep in her bed in our house, unsuspecting and alone, with no one to protect her when the monsters came. I couldn't fail. I *couldn't*.

I had a headache. It was too much. I had made a world just for me, and it had been taken from me, and transformed by a monster, and now it was up to me to save it. It was too much.

It was only when Ashwini's eyes dropped to my hand that I noticed the pitiful state of my thumbnail. I forced myself to stop. She looked like she wanted to ask me about it, but, kindly, she didn't.

Instead, she said, 'Let's take this tray out to the others, shall we?'

We went back to the front room, where the rest of the Crows were. There were books everywhere. Even Simha, the lion, had one open in front of him.

'Any luck?' Ashwini asked.

'There are no spells in the witch's spellbook that will make Kiki fly,' Suki said, closing an enormous tome with a clomp of dust.

'There are absolutely no clues about how to

defeat the palace in any of the old kings' diaries,' said Jojo.

'There are no maps of Mysore Palace in the atlas,' said Samara.

'I didn't bother to read anything,' said Pip cheerfully. 'I reckon we should take some of my stink bombs to the palace and—'

'*No,*' said Ashwini.

Simha's voice rumbled from the corner. 'While I, too, feel that books are usually the correct answer to any question, I cannot help but think that in this instance, we may have to widen our search.'

'The lion makes sense,' said Lej. He gave me a slightly scornful look. 'Do *you* have any ideas yet?'

'As a matter of fact, I do,' I said.

I had no ideas.

'Well?' said Lej.

I rapidly searched the room, determined to save my pride, and my eyes landed on the book in Suki's lap.

'The Good Witch,' I blurted.

'Who?' Pip asked, perking up with interest.

'There's a witch in Mysore,' I said. 'The one who wrote the spellbook that Suki's holding.'

'What's her name?'

I winced. 'The Good Witch.'

'Why am I not surprised?' Lej rolled his eyes. 'After all, we *are* in the presence of a lion who is literally called Lion.'

'If you could resist making fun of my creative choices for two minutes,' I said, somewhat testily, 'maybe you'd realise that this is a good idea? The reason Mysore Palace became a maze of traps after the royal family died is because one of the kings from forever ago got a witch to put a protection spell on it. The Good Witch isn't the same witch, but she may be able to undo the protection spell.'

'I suppose it's worth a try,' Ashwini said, a little doubtfully. 'Do you know where she is?'

'No,' I admitted. 'I only doodled her one time and then pretty much forgot about her until I saw the spellbook.'

Simha stretched and rose to his feet. He really was an enormous creature, with paws the size of my head and a yawn that could have swallowed me whole. 'I will go into the city and talk to the people,' he said. 'If this witch exists, someone will know where we can find her.'

'Shouldn't we all go?' I asked. 'We'll find her faster if we split up.'

'Absolutely *not*,' Ashwini said at once. 'The whole of Mahishasura's army is out there looking for you, Kiki. You can't risk being seen until we're absolutely sure we can get to that statue.'

'And I would prefer to go alone, in any case,' said Simha. 'I can travel much faster without you humans slowing me down.'

I wanted to do *something* to ease the scratchy, tireless anxiousness building and building inside me, but I knew she was right. So Simha bounded alone into the evening, leaving us behind.

'Right,' Ashwini said when he was gone. 'While we wait for him to come back, we can get some practice in.'

Suki and Pip groaned, but their groans subsided the instant Ashwini scowled at them both.

I frowned. 'Practice?'

'Battling Asuras,' said Samara. 'Ashwini makes us practice every day.'

'I have a bump on my head the size of a small country to prove it,' Suki informed me.

Ashwini continued to scowl. 'Better that than dead,' she snapped. 'I can't keep you all alive every second of every day, you know! You have to be able to protect yourselves.'

Suki bit her lip. 'I know. I'm sorry.'

'Come on, up to the roof,' Ashwini said more gently, relenting. 'You too, Kiki.'

I followed her, wondering what new disaster I was about to walk into.

12

In the corner of the kitchen, behind a blue door, was a small, rickety wooden elevator. There was only room for Jojo and one other person inside, so once he'd wheeled himself in, Pip and Suki dived forward and elbowed each other to get in next.

Suki won. 'Better luck next time,' she said cheekily, and pulled the door firmly shut. I tried very hard not to giggle at the look of sheer outrage on Pip's face.

As the elevator rattled upwards, the rest of us took the stairs.

I had been more than a little bewildered by the idea that it would be safe to practice fighting Asuras on the roof, where, presumably, the Asuras in question could easily see us, but I needn't have worried: as soon as we reached the top of a small set of spiral stairs and pushed open a trapdoor in the ceiling, I saw that the rooftop was completely hidden.

'Welcome to the Crows' Nest,' Pip said to me, grinning.

And it was very much like a nest. The rooftop's floor was made up of dark brown tiles, and it was surrounded and covered by a canopy of thick vines, trellises and plants. Bright gold shafts of late-afternoon sunlight spilt in through the gaps between the leaves and vines, and the shade made it feel cool and breezy up there in spite of the day's heat.

Jojo and Suki were already there, both examining a flower on one of the vines. 'I'm sure it's a lotus,' Suki was saying.

'But they don't grow on vines,' Jojo objected.

'This is our Mysore, Jojo. *Anything* is possible!'

Up against the sides of the rooftop were a handful of shelves, tables, planks of wood and a workbench. There were mats stacked on one side, like the kind I'd seen Emily use in her gymnastics classes, and two squishy armchairs identical to the one in the front room downstairs.

'This is amazing!' I said. 'I bet picnics up here are incredible.'

Lej raised his eyebrows. 'We don't come up here for picnics.'

'Oh.'

'OK,' Ashwini said, putting her hands on her hips. 'Let's get to work! There's a *slightly* stale and *very* delicious cake waiting for us when we're done.'

As the others whooped, I looked closer at the shelves. I could see shields and swords and spears, some made of steel, some made of wood, some clunky, some shiny, a collection as mismatched and messy as we were. Ashwini and Lej had their swords with them, but the others immediately split off to different parts of the room to get their own weapons off the shelves, like they were parts of a machine and they knew exactly what role to play.

Jojo wheeled himself to a bow and a set of crooked arrows on one of the lower shelves, while Suki snatched up a rusty woodcutter's axe and Samara picked up a simple knife. Pip debated for a while between a sword and a witch's wand before finally settling on the wand.

Suddenly, my heart felt odd and heavy, like someone had dropped a stone into the middle of it and made it sink. *This* was the life I had given them?

Battles and swords and rebel kids had seemed like such cool ideas when I was putting them in a sketchbook, like I was creating my own version of a Teen Titans movie with a heaped tablespoon of my own family's folklore, but it didn't feel cool in real life. The silver sheen of sharp steel was scary, not exciting. The violence wasn't fun.

I had made Ashwini an Asura slayer because it had seemed like a fierce, adventurous life for her on paper, but now she was stuck in that life. They all were. I loved that they were all so brave, but it didn't seem fair that they had to be brave every single day of their lives.

'What's the matter?' Ashwini said, coming up beside me. Her face, which had the Kallira nose and Gramps's straight, dark eyebrows, was anxious. 'Are you OK?'

'You're real now,' I said. 'I picked this life for all of you, but I'm not the one telling your stories any more. So how come you can't choose something else? How come none of you have picked a different life to live? You can't actually *like* this?'

'Of course we don't like it,' she said, and her tone sounded so much like Mum when she was telling me off that I felt instantly chastised. 'But we've never known any other life. We were all little when we lost our families. For years, all we've had is each other and all we know how to do is fight back.'

I noticed that she kept saying *we*. 'What about them?' I said in a low voice. 'Have you asked them if this is what *they* want?'

'I've looked after them for years, Kiki,' she snapped. 'You've been here for a few hours. What makes you think you know what they want?'

I flushed. 'I'm sorry. You're right, that wasn't fair.'

'No, *I'm* sorry,' she said, her face crumpling. 'I shouldn't have snapped at you. I know you're only asking these questions because you care about us, but I need you to trust that I'm doing what's best for all of us.'

'I do trust that! And I shouldn't have said what I did. It's a *good* thing, that you fight back. It's brave and wonderful of you.' I bit my lip. 'I just wish there was a way to beat the monsters without a sword.'

'Well, I can tell you this much,' she said more cheerfully. 'When you're up at the top of Mysore Palace, trying to break the gandaberunda's golden eye while Asuras surround you and try to stop you, you'll be glad you have a sword in your hands.'

My eyes widened. 'I don't think it's a good idea to put a sword in my hands. I'm really good at sketching swords, but not good at actually *using* them.'

'How do you know that if you've never even picked one up?' Ashwini countered. 'You have to try, Kiki. They'll come after us when we're up there and they'll tear us off that statue if we let them. You need to be able to defend yourself.'

Mahishasura flashed across my mind. The flare of his nostrils, the growl of his voice. The way his cruel eyes glittered when he made the old man break the coconuts just because he could.

If he ever gets hold of me, I won't stand a chance. If the winged Asuras of his army come after me while I'm on top of Mysore Palace, I won't stand a chance. And if I fail, what will happen to Pip and Ashwini and the other Crows? What will happen to Mum?

But if I had *something* to protect myself with ...

'OK,' I said. 'OK, I'll give it a go.'

'That's more like it,' Ashwini beamed at me. 'And if it makes you feel any better, there are tons of different weapons here. If a sword isn't right for you, chances are something else will be!'

That made sense, didn't it? After all, with so many

options, chances *were* that I'd be good at using one of them.

But, because this was me, that was not the case.

If my life had been a movie, the next two hours would have been the Dramatic Training Montage part. Like Mulan training to become a soldier, or Captain Marvel discovering what she could really do with her powers, this scene was Kiki Kallira Learning to Become a Warrior. And while I had hoped it would be an inspiring scene with awesome music, in reality it was more like a panel in a comic book where the main character falls flat on their face with an action bubble next to them saying SPLAT!

Because, as it turned out, I was absolutely, unquestionably, unbelievably *terrible* at the whole warrior thing.

The first arrow I tried to fire almost took out Lej's eye. And he was *behind* me. I cut myself when I tried to use a knife. The soft practice ball I tried to fire from a slingshot went the wrong way and hit me in the face. I dropped Suki's axe and it was only dumb luck, everyone agreed, that it missed my big toe when it clunked on to the ground. I picked up the witch's wand to turn a book into a pebble and turned Pip into a monkey instead. I couldn't even *lift* the swords. And it's probably best I don't mention what happened when I reached for a trident.

By the time I had tried and failed to use my twenty-second weapon, I was surrounded by wide eyes and slack jaws. Even Lej, who had had serious doubts about me from the moment we met, looked shocked.

'It's OK,' Ashwini said weakly. 'Practice makes perfect.'

Monkey Pip made an alarmed *ooh-ooh ah-ah* sound that left us in no doubt whatsoever about his views on letting me practise any more. Suki made the mistake of giggling and was immediately sent to the corner of the roof to search the witch's spellbook for a way to turn Pip back into himself.

'Don't worry, Kiki,' said little Samara, giving me a kind pat on the shoulder. 'This doesn't come easily to everyone. Ashwini is a natural at this stuff, but I'm not. It's OK that you aren't, either.'

I was pretty sure I had never been so embarrassed in my life, but I ignored the blush flaming up my neck and said, 'There has to be some other way I can be useful.'

This was obviously too much for Lej. 'The way you

were supposed to be useful,' he snapped, 'was by getting to the top of that palace and breaking that statue's eye. How will you do that if you can't fight off whatever comes for you while you're up there?'

I was already furious with myself, so it was very easy to transfer that fury to him. I glared at him. 'Is there anything I can do that *would* make you happy? You've been horrible to me since I got here. I'm doing my best. I'm not *trying* to be bad at this.'

'No, that part comes naturally to you,' he retorted.

'Lej,' Ashwini protested.

'She needs to hear this,' he said. His eyes flashed at me. 'I don't think you understand that no matter what happens, we can't win.'

I objected, 'Of course we can win.'

'Not you,' he said bitterly. 'Us. *We* can't win. You can go home anytime you like. We have nowhere else to go. If you fail, we'll be stuck here with the monster you set free. And if you do break that eye and banish him, well, we disappear, too, don't we? So why are you surprised that I haven't fallen over myself to be nice to you? We have to give up everything to stop Mahishasura. All *you* have to do is break a piece of stone. And apparently you can't even do that.'

I could practically see smoke coming out of Ashwini's ears. Pip, who was back in his human body, scowled at Lej. The rooftop had gone so quiet that I could hear the rumble of a drill somewhere in the distance. It hurt my head. I swallowed and tried to speak, but nothing came out.

Then, without warning, there was a *thud* above us.

Everyone froze. Ashwini's grip tightened on her sword. Her eyes landed on me and she pressed a finger to her lips.

The warning was unnecessary. I didn't think I could make a sound even if I wanted to.

I stayed absolutely still, except for my face, which tipped against my will so that I was looking directly up at the canopy of vines and leaves. A winged silhouette loomed above, completely blocking out the sun.

An Asura had landed on the canopy. My heart pounded.

'It's OK,' Pip whispered in my ear. I felt his small hand wrap around my slightly smaller one. 'They don't know we're here because the house keeps us hidden. They can't hear us, or see us, or smell us.'

'They can smell *you*,' Suki couldn't resist whispering back. 'Remember what happened last time?'

Pip looked offended. 'I told you, that was a stink bomb!'

'A likely tale.'

'Both of you shut up,' Ashwini hissed. 'How many times do I have to tell you we can't keep testing the limits of the house's power? Just stay still and stay quiet.'

I watched the shadow above us. The Asura was very still, as if it were waiting for something. Panic climbed up my throat, choking me. Did it know we were here? Did it know *I* was here? In spite of everything Pip had said, I couldn't stop myself from wondering if maybe the house's power wouldn't work on me. If maybe the monsters would always be able to find me, no matter what.

Suddenly, the Asura struck. There was a shrill squawk, and then there was silence.

The Asura flew into the sky.

Still, I didn't move. I was too busy watching a sparrow's feather drift down from the canopy.

It could so easily have been a crow.

13

Fat and golden, the moon hung low in the sky. The Kaveri sparkled underneath it and the jewel-bright rooftops of the city glowed, from the narrowest house to the opulent domes of Mysore Palace. Even my pastel castle in the clouds was lit up like it had swallowed the moon whole.

The city was so beautiful that all I wanted to do was draw it. Which was kind of weird because it only looked like this because I had *already* drawn it.

My unicorn pyjamas were in the wash, and I was pretty sure my pencil had accidentally ended up in there with them, but I had all the art stuff the house had given me. I crossed my little room to the desk in the corner and found a couple of sheets of thick watercolour paper, a box of coloured pencils and one black-ink pen. My hands longed to draw, and not just because the view outside my window was so amazing, but because my brain needed to stop thinking about what happened up on the rooftop.

But before I could get started, I heard a low thud outside my bedroom door, the squeak of wheels and a girl's voice saying, 'Shhhh!' louder than any of the other sounds. How many of the Crows were out there?

'Hello?' I said curiously.

The door opened and Pip, Jojo and the twins came in and unceremoniously shut the door behind them. Suki had a tray laden with cups of hot chocolate and a box of Mysore pak. She set it down on the floor and the four of them made themselves comfortable in various parts of the room. I watched silently, baffled.

'The others are asleep,' Pip said cheerfully, as if that explained why *they* weren't.

'Here,' said Suki, thrusting a cup at me. 'It's the best hot chocolate you'll ever have! The secret is chili powder.'

'Thanks,' I said, still confused. 'Why are you all still up? It's late.'

'Well,' said Jojo, as Suki slurped noisily at her hot chocolate, 'we got the impression that Vishnu and Lej made you feel pretty bad today. So we decided you could do with a little cheering up.'

'And a gentle reminder that they don't know everything and you shouldn't listen to them,' Pip added merrily.

Their unexpected kindness made my chest feel tight. Fireflies twinkled outside the window, and I watched them so that I didn't have to look any of the others in the eye. 'But they weren't wrong.'

'I used to be like you, you know,' Samara said unexpectedly. 'When Ashwini first found Suki and me, and we came here, I felt like I didn't fit in at all. I wasn't good at fighting. Lej tried to teach me how to go out and scavenge stuff, but I just slowed him down. I couldn't figure out plants and potions like Suki, or make cool costumes and armour like Jojo, or even build the kinds of weird devices and gadgets Pip comes up with. The only thing I was good at was reading and, well, it didn't seem like a useful thing to be good at. I felt small and weak, and I hated it.'

'That's not true,' I objected. 'You are admittedly pretty little, but you're not weak.'

She smiled. 'I know that now, but back then, I didn't get it. And that's why I know how you feel right now,

Kiki, and you need to remember that you're not weak, either. We may be little, but we're not *small*.'

'Tell Kiki what happened in the forest,' Suki said, clapping her hands with all the glee of someone about to hear a story they love.

Samara's cheeks turned a little pink, but she said, 'About a year ago, I tried to be helpful by going out to the forest on the other side of the Kaveri and finding berries, mushrooms, that kind of stuff. All I took with me was an empty basket, a book and an apple as a snack. While I was out there, a wolf Asura found me. I ran, but I'm not very fast and I knew he'd catch me.'

The others were all grinning, watching me as I watched Samara, riveted. 'And then?' I asked.

'I remembered something I'd read in one of my books,' she replied. 'Asuras need to eat meat to survive, but wolf Asuras can't resist the smell of apple juice. I have no idea why that is, but it's what saved me that day. I pulled out my apple and started biting off bits of it. I spat them out on to the forest floor as I ran, making a trail for the wolf to follow. I led him right into an old hunter's trap.'

'And then she was sick all over her shoes,' Suki couldn't resist adding.

Her twin grinned. 'It's true. And when I got back home, I was sick all over Suki's shoes, too.'

I laughed, but my brain replayed the story. There was something so brilliant and hopeful about Samara finding out that the thing she loved, the *one* thing she knew she was good at, was actually every bit as useful as anything any of the others could do.

'I know what you're trying to say,' I said. 'You're saying I shouldn't let Vishnu or Lej decide what I'm capable of. I should decide for myself.'

'And you shouldn't let them tell you how you should fight back,' Jojo added. 'You can't fight monsters like anyone else. You can only fight monsters like *you*.'

Along with myths and stories and lullabies, Mum would read me poems when I was little. One of those poems was by a man called William Ernest Henley. There were two lines at the end of the poem that went like this:

> *I am the master of my fate,*
> *I am the captain of my soul.*

That was what they were all trying to tell me. They were telling me to be the master of my own fate.

But it wasn't that easy. How could I not take what Vishnu had said to heart when I knew he was right? He hadn't said anything that I hadn't already said to myself over the past couple of years. I *was* an anxious little girl who wanted her hand held. I *was* a little girl who could hold a pencil, but not a sword.

'Sometimes I still doubt myself,' Samara said, like she could hear what I was thinking. 'Then I see the books on my shelves, and I remember that I outsmarted a wolf.'

I smiled. 'You bet you did.'

She reached over and squeezed my hand. 'It's OK to be scared,' this kind, smart little girl said. 'We all are.'

I clutched my cup tighter. 'I don't know how to beat *my* big bad wolf.'

'That's because you've let yourself believe that there's only one way to do it,' Pip pointed out. 'But a sword isn't the only way to fight, Kiki.'

It was true, of course. Every room in this house, and every Crow in it, was proof of that. Hope unfurled inside me, like a small flower reaching for the sun.

'I don't think drawing pictures is going to help me stop Mahishasura,' I said. 'And I can't think of anything else I'm especially good at, but if I can't find a way to the top of Mysore Palace and break the gandaberunda's eye, I'm going to have to figure out another way to beat him.'

'Potions are very useful,' Suki said. 'I can teach you how to make them!'

'We can *all* teach you,' Jojo chimed in. 'We're all good at different things. We can all help you.'

Pip beamed. 'I'll have you making the stinkiest stink bomb in no time!'

'I've seen you make a firework out of matchsticks and some chewing gum,' Suki said to him. 'I'm pretty sure you can do better than those terrible stink bombs.'

'They're *supposed* to be terrible—'

'We'll all help you, Kiki,' Samara said quietly. 'But you shouldn't give up on the idea of using what you're already good at, either. Books saved me. Maybe your art will save you.'

'It helped me in the real world,' I admitted. 'On the other hand, it also helped Mahishasura escape the Nowhere Place. My sketchbook is the reason you have to spend your lives fighting him.'

Pip turned to me. 'Oh, hey, I wanted to ask. Why'd you call us the Crows?'

'I like them,' I said a little sheepishly. 'A lot of people think they're noisy and a nuisance, but they're actually really loyal and smart.'

'To be fair, we *are* noisy,' Suki pointed out, giggling.

'And you and Pip are definitely a nuisance,' Jojo added with a straight face.

'Hey!'

'There's this story that they tell where my granddad is from,' I went on. 'They say that when people die, they don't leave the world straightaway. Instead, they become crows, and they stay for a while to make sure the people they loved are OK.'

'I like that,' Pip said happily. 'Maybe all the crows in the world are actually the souls of loving, loyal people. Wouldn't that be nice?'

Jojo put his empty cup back down on the tray. 'We'd better go to bed,' he said a little reluctantly.

'Thank you for this,' I said as the others stretched and got to their feet. 'It was really kind of you.'

'It seemed like you needed a friend,' said Pip, with that sweet, joyful smile. 'So we decided to bring you four.'

Warmth spread across my body, lifting my heart up out of the dark place it had been swallowed by. One by one, my new (and old) friends crept out of my room. Suki was the last one to go. With her hand on my doorknob, she paused and looked back at me.

'Try to remember, OK?'

'Remember what?'

'Little girls *can* beat big bad wolves. We have teeth, too.'

14

The next day, the warmth was gone. As I picked at my toast and looked at the others around the breakfast table, from Ashwini making sure everyone had plenty to eat to Simha drinking his tea out of a ludicrously tiny cup, I felt cold and horrible.

Once the gandaberunda's eye was broken, this Mysore would be gone. *They* would all be gone. Simha, who loved his tea and had chosen to stay here to protect me. These kids, who had been so kind to me and were so brave. All gone. Banishing Mahishasura would mean losing them all.

And I knew this world was never supposed to exist. I knew that. But it was still hard to think about it *un-*existing again.

There was a Mysore that had once been beautiful. The one I had created before I'd introduced Mahishasura to it. The Mysore of circuses and kings and joy, where kids like Suki could grow flowers instead of poisons. I remembered the full, lively streets, the festivals, the jewel houses echoing with happy voices, the kids who got to be kids. I knew there was no such thing as a perfect world in real life, but my Mysore *had* been perfect before Mahishasura.

And now it would never get the chance to be beautiful again. The quiet, ghostly streets outside, the frightened old man with his coconuts, the hurried footsteps, the fear, the monsters in the sky – that was all the people would ever know. The Crows would never do anything but fight. I couldn't give any of them a happy ending.

Only an ending.

'Kiki,' Pip whispered beside me.

I looked up, startled. His eyes were on my hands. I looked down and saw that they were clenched around my slice of toast, ripping it into tinier and tinier shreds.

I made myself let go. Pip looked worried. 'Are you OK?'

'I'm fine,' I said, forcing a smile. I put my hands

under the table and squashed them under my thighs to keep them still.

'I'll be out for most of the day,' Ashwini said brightly, getting everyone's attention. 'And Lej will be in and out as well, so can I trust the rest of you to keep yourselves from getting captured or eaten while we're gone?'

'You have no reason to worry,' Pip said, in the kind of tone that promised mischief and many reasons for Ashwini to worry. 'We'll be good.'

Ashwini eyed him askance, but clearly decided it wasn't worth the time or energy to question this.

'Where are you going?' I asked. 'Can I help?'

'No, you cannot,' said Pip, before either Ashwini or Lej could even open their mouths. '*You* have lessons. Here. With us.'

'I'm not going to ask,' Ashwini said, looking slightly concerned. Then she added, 'I'm going to the Witches' Guild. They're pretty hard to get to, but if I *can* find them, they may be able to point me in the direction of the Good Witch. Simha didn't have any luck yesterday.'

'It seems humans do not respond well to lions asking questions,' said Simha huffily.

'Not entirely without reason,' Lej pointed out.

'Hmpf.'

'And I'm heading over to the metalworkers' quarter,' Lej went on. 'Someone there may know how to craft a pair of mechanical wings.'

I looked up in alarm. 'I wasn't serious when I said we could fly to the top of the palace, you know.'

'Sometimes you have halfway decent ideas,' said Lej, and then ruined the almost compliment by adding, 'even if you seem to only come up with them by accident.'

'OK, out,' Ashwini said hastily, probably afraid we'd have a repeat of yesterday's battle. She got to her feet and hauled Lej to the door with her. 'You have places to be, and so do I.' She hesitated, glancing back at me. 'Stay put, OK?'

I didn't know if that was her way of reminding me to be careful, or her way of pleading with me not to abandon them, but either way, my answer was the same.

'I'll be here,' I promised her.

She smiled, and was gone.

What if she didn't come back?

It wasn't a question I *wanted* to think about, but my brain didn't listen. It went straight there, conjuring thoughts that I didn't want and couldn't avoid. I looked down at my hands. The nail on my left thumb had a bit more of the white at the end than the others. Just the teeniest nibble would make it match the rest …

'We don't *have* to teach you stuff today, Kiki,' Suki said, jerking my attention away from my hands. 'Your world pretty much turned upside down yesterday, so if you want to just do nothing today, that's totally OK.'

I shook my head. 'I need to do my part. And I have to keep my brain busy anyway.' I couldn't force my brain to stop thinking the things I didn't want it to, but sometimes, if I was lucky, I could replace the not-nice stuff by finding something more fun to become obsessed with instead.

My sketchbook used to be that fun thing, but that wasn't exactly an option when I was, you know, *inside* it.

'OK!' Suki said happily. 'Pip and I are going to bite into an oobly-floobly to decide who gets to give you your first lesson.'

Simha, who had started washing up the breakfast dishes by licking them, looked up. 'That seems unwise,' he remarked.

'That's pretty much the story of their lives,' Samara informed him.

'I'm sorry,' I said. 'Suki, did you just say you and Pip are going to *bite* an ooble-flooble? Do I want to know what an ooble-flooble is?'

'Oobly-floobly,' Pip corrected as Suki reached across the sink to the kitchen windowsill, where a row of small potted plants were lined up. She picked up one of them, a succulent of some sort.

'This,' said Suki triumphantly, 'is an oobly-floobly. Do you see the tiny nodules on each leaf? There is a fifty-fifty chance that, when touched, the nodules will burst and release a horrid, bitter *goo*. So Pip and I are going to bite down on the leaves! The first one to taste the bitter goo gets to give you your first lesson.'

'None of that makes sense!'

'Also the story of their lives,' Samara said.

Jojo covered his eyes, his dark brown skin taking on something of a greenish hue. 'I can't watch.'

A grin crept across my face. 'I am absolutely going to watch!'

In the end, after much fanfare, Pip had the debatable good fortune of bursting a nodule first. But the bitter goo was so horrible that he had to spend twenty minutes literally washing his mouth out with soap, so Suki seized the opportunity to whisk me up to her room for my first lesson, while Pip's yells of *'Cheat!'* followed us up the stairs.

'You know,' I said to Suki, 'a suspicious person might wonder if you knew just how bad the oobly-floobly would taste and you lured Pip right into a trap, you being the plant person and all.'

Suki blinked innocently at me. 'Are *you* a suspicious person?'

I bit back a giggle. 'No matter what this lesson is about,' I warned her, 'I'm *not* licking anything.'

And that was pretty much how the day went. Pip and Suki tried to one-up each other every chance they got, Jojo and Samara did their best to ignore them and played *Giants & Gargoyles* instead, and Simha appeared to be deeply regretting his decision to stick with us.

But between it all, I started to learn. Suki showed me how to crush the petals of an iridescent purple flower to make a healing potion. I helped Jojo sew threads of starlight into the Crows' costumes ('For that extra bit of protection,' he explained). Samara loaned me a book called *When You Can't Beat Monsters, Trick Them*, with helpful sections marked with sticky notes. And, surrounded by the made-up adventures of my childhood, Pip and I made stink bombs, balloons filled with the oobly-floobly's bitter goo and mechanical insects ('They're *very* distracting!').

Even Simha, who hadn't exactly signed up to be both babysitter *and* tutor, took a break from attempting to bake a loaf of focaccia to offer me a lesson.

'What,' he said, opening his jaws very wide, a mere inch from my face, 'does my breath smell like?'

In the pursuit of good manners, I tried very hard not to gag. (One could argue that it was hardly good manners to open one's jaws and blow hot, carnivorous breath upon unsuspecting humans, but I wasn't about to debate this point with a lion.)

'Um,' I said, as diplomatically as possible. 'Is it meat?'

'The correct answer,' Simha rumbled, 'is that what it smells like is irrelevant. If you can smell the breath of a creature my size, it is already too late.'

'Thanks for sharing that extremely new piece of information,' I said. 'I'll do my best not to put my head inside the maws of any lions, demons or bears.'

'There are no bears in Mysore,' said Simha, and stalked back to the kitchen to check on his focaccia.

I kept myself busy, but in the quiet moments, I

wondered if Mum was OK. I missed her and wished she could have come here with me, so that she could have been sensible and funny and kind and grown-up, but mostly, I couldn't get away from the familiar fear that something terrible would happen to her. I tried repeatedly to remind myself that, for one, she was still fast asleep in her bed and time had not moved forward for her, and, for another, Ashwini had assured me that nothing else could get out of my sketchbook. Yet. But I was me, so I worried anyway.

Ashwini and Lej came back late that afternoon, both safe and sound. Neither had had any luck finding either the Witches' Guild or a metalworker who could make me fly, but when the others told Ashwini how much I'd learnt over the course of the day, she perked right up and insisted on giving me lessons, too.

'That didn't work out so well yesterday,' I reminded her.

'No weapons this time,' she said cheerfully. 'I'm going to teach you other stuff first. Like how to find an Asura's heart if it's not in the usual place. Or how to poke the fleshy part in an Asura's armpit just *so* to make it let you go.'

So that was what we did, at least until Suki wailed up the stairs to us that she was absolutely *starving* and could Ashwini *please* come and fix the mess Lej was making of dinner?

As Ashwini stomped downstairs to do just that, I couldn't help noticing that she looked exhausted.

'I'll make dinner,' I offered. 'I make really good cheese toasties!'

So we all ate cheese toasties, and then we shared what was left of yesterday's stale, but still perfectly nice, chocolate cake, and Lej and I didn't murder each other, so it was, all in all, a pretty good day.

The night wasn't as good. I dreamt of Mahishasura. He was waiting for me on top of a white throne, but when I got closer, I saw that his throne was made up of Mum, Emily and the Crows, all frozen in marble.

'You failed them all,' said the demon king. 'You were weak and afraid, and now I have won.'

I woke up shaking. It was still dark outside, but I knew I wouldn't get back to sleep, so I picked up *When You Can't Beat Monsters, Trick Them* and read it until the sun came up and Pip came bounding into my room to fetch me for breakfast.

*

The next three days had an almost comforting pattern: forced to stay put until Ashwini found us a way to the gandaberunda, I spent my time on plants and potions with Suki, traps and tomfoolery with Pip, books with Samara, enchanted tailoring with Jojo and more dubious lessons from Simha. Before dinner, Ashwini showed me a number of ways to defend myself, many of which seemed to involve armpits, and then, when the others had gone to bed, Pip and I would stay up to play *Giants & Gargoyles*, read books that weren't about monsters and talk about the adventures we had back when he was still imaginary.

I spent a lot of the time gazing out of the windows of Crow House and looking at the kingdom I'd made and broken. Those were the not-good moments; the moments when I wondered if maybe it wouldn't matter that I'd learnt how to sew sunbeams into fabric and brew a potion that could freeze a small creature in its tracks. What was the point of any of it if I couldn't do the *one* thing these kids and this city really needed from me?

Then, on my fifth day in my sketchbook world, Ashwini came home with news. 'I found the Witches' Guild,' she said triumphantly.

Suki clapped her hands in excitement. 'Did they tell you about the Good Witch?'

'I haven't seen them yet,' said Ashwini. 'I just know where they'll be at dawn tomorrow. I spoke to someone who knows someone who says that a couple of witches from the guild will be at the black market in Tamarind Station.'

It took me a second to pick that sentence apart. 'So you should be able to go to this market at dawn and find the guild?'

'Exactly,' said Ashwini.

'But?' Lej prompted from the corner of the room, where he lurked like an evil omen.

'How did you know there was a *but*?'

'There's always a *but*.'

'There is a *teensy* catch,' Ashwini admitted. 'Apparently, they won't talk to me. They'll only talk to Kiki. Which means you're going to have to come to the black market with me.'

15

At dawn, with only a sliver of sunlight in the pinkish sky, Ashwini and I left Crow House with Chamundeshwari. We'd all agreed that letting Simha come with us would attract too much attention, so he had suggested Chamundeshwari instead. No one was *expecting* to find trouble at this mysterious black market (at least, I hoped not!), but any time I spent outside the protection of the house carried a risk that the Asuras would find me, so we'd decided it was better to be safe than sorry.

'This is a secret underground market that's always held at dawn in Tamarind Station,' Ashwini told me as we slipped down dim cobbled streets, dressed in drab browns like farmers and fisherwomen. 'It's held once a week, on different days, and Mahishasura has never found it. I guess the Witches' Guild must have put a protection spell over it or something.'

'Why is it secret?' I asked. 'Is it different from the other markets?'

'Mahishasura takes a *very* high tax from the other markets,' said Ashwini. 'If you want to trade in the city, you have to pretty much let Mahishasura steal from you so that he can fill Lalith Mahal with more gold and jewels. The underground market is the one place people can trade for free.'

'And it's in Tamarind Station because ...'

'It used to be a train station,' said Ashwini cheerfully. 'There's lots of space!' Then she darted forward, her sword glinting under her shabby cloak. 'I need to scout ahead and make sure our way is clear.'

As Chamundeshwari and I trailed behind her, I darted a shy look at my version of the warrior goddess. She didn't seem to speak much.

'Yes?' she said mildly.

'Thanks for letting Simha stay with us while all this is going on,' I said. 'He's been really good company.'

'Good. He likes to fuss, and he's had no one to fuss over for years other than me, so I suspect he's thrilled to be in a house full of children.'

I tried not to giggle at the idea of Simha as a helicopter parent.

'I suspect it's good for those children to be fussed over, too,' Chamundeshwari went on, her eyes narrowing on Ashwini up ahead. 'Especially that one.'

Guilt made my chest tighten, but I said, 'I don't know, I think Ashwini likes being the boss of everyone.'

'Does she?' said Chamundeshwari, shifting her solemn eyes to me. 'I think it would be difficult to be thirteen years old, a monster hunter *and* the sole protector and caretaker of several children.' Whatever she saw in my face made hers soften slightly, and she patted me on the shoulder. 'You did not know.'

After a moment, I said, 'Did I mess everything up for you, too?'

'Well,' she said gravely, 'I could do without the glitter.'

For a moment, I was mortified. Then I saw the tiny twinkle in her eye, and I sputtered a laugh. 'Sorry.'

'You should not be so quick to assume you have, as you put it, messed everything up,' she said more seriously. 'Be gentler to yourself, Kiki. You are here, are you not? That tells me you are kinder and braver than you give yourself credit for.'

A few moments later, we got on a totally out-of-place red London bus (the only one still working in Mysore, Ashwini told me) and it took us the rest of the way to Tamarind Station.

Tamarind Station was a ruin. In my Mysore-Before-Mahishasura, it had been a quaint, bright place, with impractical pastel-pink railway lines criss-crossed around it. It resembled a thatched cottage, with far more space inside than it seemed from the outside, and the platforms had all looked like little porches leading out to the tracks. The trains had been just as merry, bright and red as the bus, chugging their way up and down the city.

In Mysore-After-Mahishasura, the railway lines were buried under rubble and dust, and a handful of train cars stood abandoned on the tracks, the red faded to a dull rust. Tamarind Station was a shell, the straw roof mostly torn off, the stone walls half crumbled, the door gone.

There had been a battle here. I remembered drawing it; remembered the colours. Chamundeshwari and Simha had fought in it.

I stood still for the moment, staring at the station. At what had once been a sunshine thing, now ruined.

But then Ashwini grabbed me by the hand and trotted enthusiastically into the remains of the station, and I gasped out loud.

What was dead and ruined on the outside became astonishingly, brilliantly alive and vibrant on the inside. The old station walls had been painted a clean, bright white, the terracotta tiles on the floor gleamed and hundreds of sparkling orbs of bottled sunlight floated above our heads. There were stalls *everywhere*, selling everything from chutney, apples and rice to distilled moonbeams, spellbooks and fabric stitched out of stars.

It was too noisy and busy for me, and it kind of hurt my head, but it was also incredible to see how alive this city still was.

'Over there,' Ashwini whispered in my ear, bouncing up and down with excitement. 'See that stall? They must be from the Witches' Guild!'

The stall was simple, draped in purple silks and piled high with spellbooks, wands and bottles of sparkling potions. Two women attended to the stall; one was old and leaning on a sturdy black cane, chatting animatedly to an old man at the next stall, while the other was about twenty years old, with black hair that tumbled all the way down to her waist. She had a look of intense concentration on her face as she sat cross-legged on the floor in front of the stall with a book in her lap.

As we got nearer, her eyes suddenly snapped up and met mine. And, with unmistakable authority, she beckoned me closer.

I approached warily, with Ashwini skipping along beside me. Chamundeshwari followed us.

The young witch made no move to rise, but simply tipped her head back to look up at me. 'Statue girl,' she said.

'Witch lady?' I replied, somewhat doubtfully.

That made her mouth twitch, but she only said, 'You look like your statue.'

'We were told you'd only talk to Kiki,' Ashwini said. 'So here she is. At no small risk to herself, by the way.'

'It's OK,' I said quickly. 'I wanted to come. We, um, we need your help.'

'So we assumed, from how persistently your friend over there has been trying to find us,' said the witch drily. Having studied me at length, she lowered her head and turned back to her book. 'What can we do for you?'

'There's a protection spell on Mysore Palace,' I said, slightly unnerved at having to ask the top of her head for a favour. 'We were hoping one of you might be able to undo it.'

'That protection spell was placed by one of our ancestors, back when our power was far greater,' said the witch, licking a fingertip and turning a page. 'The only one of us alive today who *might* be able to undo such a spell is the Good Witch.'

I nodded. It would have been convenient if one of these two witches could have done it themselves, but I'd expected this. 'Do you know where we can find her?'

'You're out of luck, I'm afraid,' said the witch. 'She's been a prisoner of Mahishasura's for weeks. If you want her, you'll have to go to Lalith Mahal and help her escape.'

Ashwini and I stood in total silence for a moment, crushed. 'But,' I protested, 'we can't go to Lalith Mahal. That's his *fortress*. And if we can't undo the protection spell, we may not be able to banish him and ...' I trailed off, knowing it was no use. She couldn't do anything about it. So I took a deep breath and remembered my manners. 'Thank you for answering my questions. That was all we wanted, so I guess we'll go now.'

'This is just a teeny setback,' Ashwini said to me, recovering quickly. 'We'll work it out, and we'll get to the top of that palace, one way or another.'

'If he doesn't find you first,' said the witch.

At this, Chamundeshwari spoke up. 'If you know something we do not,' she said sternly, 'the very least you can do is share that information rather than use it to taunt a child.'

The witch looked up from her book. 'It was not intended as a taunt, goddess,' she said, offended. 'Mahishasura is looking for the child. You know that already. Take care that he cannot find her.'

'Our house keeps her hidden,' Ashwini said.

The witch cocked her head to one side. 'Yes, but it cannot hide her from a powerful tracking spell. Given that Mahishasura is holding the Good Witch prisoner, he could force her to perform the spell on one of the child's possessions. It would lead him straight to her, no matter where she is.'

'Well, that's not a problem,' Ashwini said brightly. 'He doesn't have any of Kiki's possessions. She's barely been outside Crow House and you haven't lost anything, right, Kiki?'

'No,' I said at once. 'I still have everything I came

here with – it was just the clothes I was wearing, and my pencil obviously, and ...'

I stopped short as sudden realisation and horror swept over me.

'What is it?' Chamundeshwari asked.

In my mind, I could see a fire, and then nothing where the fire had been, and then wet wood.

'My desk,' I said softly. 'My curtains. The demon set them on fire in London. Then Ashwini pushed them through the tear to make sure the fire didn't spread through my bedroom, so they're here, in *this* world. And if Mahishasura has them ...'

'Yes,' said the witch, with some sympathy. 'If he has them, he can find you.'

16

'This is not a problem,' Ashwini insisted, as we took the bus back to the southwest of the city. She sounded so completely certain that I almost believed her, and I definitely *wanted* to believe her, but I wasn't quite there. 'You've been here for a few days now, Kiki. If Mahishasura had forced the Good Witch to use your desk or curtains to perform a locator spell, he would have found you by now. And if he hasn't done it already, it must be because it either hasn't occurred to him or he hasn't been able to find a possession of yours. After all,' she went on, rocketing ahead before I could object, 'why would the Asuras look twice at some burnt rags and wood? They're focused on *you*. They're not looking for possessions you may have left behind on that balcony.'

'We could find out for sure,' I said. 'If we go back to the tear and find my stuff still there, we'll know they haven't used any of it and we can get rid of it all. And if we can't find it, well, we'll still know more than we do now, won't we?'

'That's a *huge* risk for something that doesn't really matter,' Ashwini said.

'Doesn't really matter? If they find me, they'll find all of you, too. Crow House won't be able to protect any of you any more!'

'They won't find any of us,' Ashwini insisted. 'I'm telling you, I know what Mahishasura's like. If he hasn't used a locator spell already, he's not going to.'

'It would be better to make sure—'

'We cannot go back to the tear, Kiki,' Chamundeshwari cut in gently. 'I am sorry. It is heavily guarded. Even I cannot get near it, or else I would have gone, I promise you.'

My shoulders slumped back into the hard bus seat. 'There has to be a way.'

'Kiki, let it go,' Ashwini said, her tone both bossy and kind. 'I know you're worried, but it'll be OK. I won't let anything happen to you or the others.'

I bit my lip, but I said nothing. How could I explain?

How could I tell her that I wasn't just worried? Worrying was bearable. Even fear was bearable. But the horrible scratchy feeling inside my brain was not.

I knew how to make it stop. I had to go see if my desk and curtains were still next to the tear or if Mahishasura had taken them to track me down. Once I knew for sure that we were all safe – the Crows, Mum and I – then the Something that was in my brain wouldn't scratch at me any more.

And of course I couldn't do that. I couldn't go and check. Ashwini and Chamundeshwari were right; it was too risky.

So I just had to stop thinking about it.

Any second now.

I was still thinking about it.

'We have to get to the statue of the gandaberunda,' Ashwini was saying. 'Everything else is a distraction.'

But we got back to Crow House, told the other Crows what had happened and let the hours of the day go by, and still we had no way to get to the statue.

Meanwhile, I could think of nothing but my burnt desk and curtains. I was so anxious that I was a hazard to anyone who came near me. I tried to help Jojo make a glamour jacket, which would make Asura eyes slide past the wearer, and ended up ripping a hole in the fabric and wasting a whole lot of precious stardust. I tried to help Suki brew more of the freezing potion and ended up spilling some on her foot, which left it frozen in place and forced her to hop around until it wore off. I was absolutely useless in a game of *Giants & Gargoyles* with Pip, Samara and Simha. It got to a point where even Lej, who had done his best to avoid me since I'd arrived in Mysore, went out of his way to ask me who spit in my soup.

'You're the worrying sort,' I said to him. 'Don't *you* think we should go and make sure the desk and curtains are still there?'

'Yes, I do,' he said bluntly. 'I also know we can't do that, so I'm sensibly worrying about other stuff instead.'

I wished I could do the same, but it just wasn't possible. Nothing could distract me for long – not playing board games, not reading a book and not even making dosas again. The anxiety was too sharp, too persistent, and it scratched and scratched and scratched.

That night, after dinner, Ashwini dropped something of a bombshell. 'So, I've been thinking it over all day,' she said. 'And I reckon the only thing to do is go to Lalith Mahal and rescue the Good Witch.'

'What?' Jojo said incredulously. 'No way. We'd never get in, let alone get *out* again!'

'I think we can do it,' she said. 'I know it's a *tiny* bit more perilous than anything we've ever done before, but if we don't do it, how will we get to that statue?'

Lej gave a sharp jerk of his head. 'There has to be a better way to get to it.'

'And what would that better way be?' Ashwini asked him. 'Oh, you don't know? I didn't think so.'

'If we go to Lalith Mahal, we won't come back.'

'We will if we're clever.'

'Do you have a way in and out?'

'Not yet, but—'

'Then this is pointless,' Lej snapped.

I really, *really* hated agreeing with Lej, but I did. Ashwini was probably the bravest person I had ever known, and I was in awe of that, but I knew Lalith Mahal. It would be impossible to get in and out. (I had made it that way. I had had this idea that I needed to make everything really hard for the heroes so that it would be much cooler when they won. Thanks, Past Kiki. Thanks a lot.)

'What if we try Plan B?' I said quietly.

Both Ashwini and Lej stopped shouting and looked

at me. Every other head turned, too. Ashwini's brow furrowed. 'Plan B?'

'Vishnu's way,' I said, swallowing.

'The plan that involves you fighting and destroying Mahishasura?' Lej asked with an air of profound doom. '*That* plan?'

'I don't like it either, OK?' I said. 'I'm terrified. But what if it's the only way? What if it's the better way?'

Ashwini looked shocked. 'How can it be better? You can't beat him, Kiki.'

'So what you're telling us,' said Lej, 'is you think that the *better* way is for you and your silly unicorn pyjamas to battle the Asura king?'

'This may come as a surprise to you, but I really don't care that you think my pyjamas are silly,' I said. '*I* like them. And, yes, I do get that it sounds like a terrible idea. Maybe it *is* a terrible idea. But what if it works?'

'It is absolutely a terrible idea,' he said. He looked ready to pull his hair out. 'You've demonstrated a frankly implausible level of incompetence with every weapon I've had the misfortune of seeing you hold, so I have no idea what you think you'll be able to do if you go up against Mahishasura. Unless you think you can sneak up on him and smother him in his sleep, there is no way you can win. You're more likely to get yourself killed and, more importantly, get the rest of us killed with you.'

I tried very hard not to bare my teeth at him. *He* was the one who had told me just how much they stood to lose. Didn't he see that I was trying to find a way to save both our worlds *without* turning them all back into ink? Didn't he get that I was trying to keep my mother and the real world safe *without* sacrificing all of them?

Before I could stop myself, I said, 'I don't need your permission. I made this world. It's mine. You don't get to tell me what I can and can't do!'

The good news: Lej stopped scowling for the first time since I'd met him.

The bad news: he stopped scowling because he burst out laughing.

'You sound as bad as Mahishasura,' he howled. 'Except he's scary and you're ridiculous. You're a tiny tyrant, stamping your foot and screaming because you want so badly to be in control, and hate that you aren't!'

I felt my entire face burn hot and tried very hard not to look at the others. I didn't think I could bear to see the looks on their faces. 'That sounds more like a toddler than a tyrant,' I mumbled.

Still chortling, Lej turned away. 'If the shoe fits.'

'Why is it wrong to want just a little bit of control, anyway?' I demanded. 'I had it once. I was *happy*. And then one day I wasn't any more.'

He froze. Slowly, he turned back to look at me.

The words tumbled out of me. '*Thoughts* would just pop into my head and I couldn't make them stop crowding me,' I said. 'I was always obsessed with something, anxious about something. So I started spending more and more time with art and stories, because that was the only way I knew how to make my brain go quiet, and then I made this world. And for a couple of months, I was happy again. I *loved* every part of this place. Until I found out a monster had sneaked in and stolen it from me. And I couldn't stop that, either.' I scrubbed the back of my hand across my nose, trying very hard not to cry. 'So tell me why, Lej. Tell me why I should be sorry for wanting to be in control just *once*.'

Lej stared at me like he had never seen me before. He blinked a few times and shook his head like a dog shaking water out of its ears.

'Actually,' I said quickly, 'don't answer that. I don't want to hear whatever it is you have to say.'

I stood and left the kitchen, fleeing up to my room. The room this house had made me, now filled with coloured pencils and ink I hadn't even had a chance to use because I'd been so busy trying to learn something useful instead, but also crammed with odds and ends I'd got and made in my lessons with the others. It was a patchwork room, as confused as I was, and it hurt to look at it.

Soft paws thumped on the floor behind me. Then Simha brushed his enormous, warm head against my clenched fist. 'Take heart,' he rumbled. 'All will be well in the end.'

'What if it's not?'

'If it is not well, trust that it is not yet the end.'

I didn't know if that made me feel any better, but it was kind of him to try. Just as it was kind of him not to eat any of us; a generous gesture I did not take for granted. (But if he *did* want to eat someone, I was happy to point him in Lej's direction.)

'Do *you* think I could beat Mahishasura?' I asked, hating how small and unsure my voice sounded.

Simha moved closer, letting me curl one hand

into the rich, soft fur of his mane. 'Not with a sword,' he said.

'He's the king of all the Asuras,' I said. 'How do I destroy him without a sword?'

'I cannot answer that,' said the lion.

Restless, fidgety, I chewed on my thumbnail as I stared out of the window at Mysore. A world that had once been joyful was now dark and cold.

Except for places like the black market in Tamarind Station. And this house. Crow House, and everyone inside it, would turn to ink and paper if I banished Mahishasura back to the Nowhere Place. And if I didn't, if I tried to fight him instead, I'd lose and they'd be gone anyway.

But at least both of those choices *were* a choice. I could choose to banish him, or I could choose to fight him. What *wasn't* a choice was letting him find me. Letting him slip into this beautiful house and destroy everything that was good and joyful inside it.

Because if he had my desk and my curtains, he could find me. And if he found me, I could see the inevitable sequence of consequences already. They would come, probably when it was dark and quiet and everyone was asleep, and they would rip apart the doors like they were paper. Ashwini and Lej and Simha would fight, and would probably be killed, and Jojo would try to fire arrows at them, but they'd get to him, too. They'd pull the twins out of their beds, and burn Samara's beloved books and Suki's beautiful plants, and then they'd come upstairs and find Pip and me, and by that point, it wouldn't matter what we did because the house would be on fire and everyone else would be gone—

Simha let out a small yelp, and I jerked my head down to see that the hand stroking his mane had clenched into the fur.

'I'm so sorry! Are you OK?'

'Startled, mostly,' said Simha with a snort. 'It would take more than a child's overenthusiastic grip to make me not OK.'

It would take the teeth and the claws of Asuras, dozens of them, and I was watching them do just that inside my head.

'Stop,' I said. My mouth shaped the word, but no sound came out. Still, I wondered if maybe this time my brain would listen. *'Stop.'*

But it didn't stop. It went on all night, an endless cycle of gruesome consequences, and the worst part was that I couldn't even laugh and comfort myself with how silly I was being, because this wasn't sharks in swimming pools or malevolent geese. Nothing in my head was too unlikely, too far-fetched. These monsters were real, and they would come.

'Make it stop,' I said into the darkness of my room, over and over. 'Make it stop!' Maybe I hoped the house would hear me and be able to do what I couldn't. Maybe I hoped Vishnu would reappear as if by magic and say he'd help me, after all. Or maybe not. I wasn't sure what I wanted. It was hard to know when there was no space inside my head for anything other than a desk, some curtains and the monsters.

In the end, I knew only I could make it stop, and I had to. I had to do *something*. My fingers had left deep half-moons in my palms from digging my nails in so hard. My throat was raw. Even taking a breath hurt. I had to do something to make sure they couldn't find me. I had to do something to quiet the noise inside my head. I couldn't sit here and feel like this any more.

I pretended to be asleep when Pip came to get me for breakfast. I waited to hear the sound of them all in the kitchen, safely tucked away, and then I got dressed. Unicorn pyjamas and a borrowed pair of Pip's scuffed sneakers. And I knew, even as I tiptoed out of my room, that I should stay put. I knew, even as I crept down the stairs, that I should go back to bed.

But I didn't. I couldn't. It was too much.

So I slipped out of the front door and left Crow House.

17

The sun was up and blazing hot, and the air felt thick and sticky. The only person outside the house was the woman who swept the square every morning, and she paid no attention to me as I ran past her, past the statue and slipped into one of the streets. Monsters darted across the sky with the soft *shh shh shh* of wings. I ducked into doorways, trying to keep out of sight. My heart pounded.

Would I be able to find my way back to the tear between worlds? I hoped so. I had a pretty good visual memory, probably from all the time I spent creating pictures, so I was sure I could remember the way we had come.

I passed a few people, but no one tried to speak to me. They ducked their heads and walked past. I hated how quickly everyone moved, how hurriedly they spoke to each other, how fast they seemed to want to get back to their homes. I hated how afraid they were.

I spotted the banyan tree up ahead. Relieved, I headed towards it.

Then something grabbed my sleeve.

I shrieked. A human hand closed over my mouth, silencing me.

'Don't scream! It's just me!'

Pip?

I spun around. There was cold sweat all over my skin. 'You scared me half to death!'

'Sorry,' he said with that quick, mischievous grin.

'Why are you out here?'

'After last night, I knew it was only a matter of time before you'd try to find out whether Mahishasura has your stuff or not,' he replied, sounding rather pleased with himself. 'So I asked the house to tell me if you sneaked out. It did. Ta-da!'

'Well, go back,' I said. 'It's not safe out here.'

He raised his eyebrows. 'I know. That's why I'm not going back.'

'Pip,' I protested.

'Kiki.'

'Pip.'

'Kiki.'

'I don't have time to fight with you about this!'

'Good, because I'm not letting you out of my sight,' he chirped. 'Shall we go?'

I stared at him for a moment, a lump in my throat. I didn't know how to tell him that I wished he would go back, but I was also glad he wasn't. So I nodded and ducked under the branches of the banyan tree. He fell into step beside me.

'I have to know,' I said after a moment. 'I have to know if they're coming, and if they're not, I have to make sure they can't.'

'I know,' said Pip cheerfully. I waited, but not one word of criticism came out of his mouth.

We crossed a street and hurried past the open fairground. It was empty; the circus gone, the plants overgrown, stray bits of paper fluttering sadly in the dirt. My heart ached as I remembered my sketches of the circus before Mahishasura; the bright tents, the cotton candy, the joy.

Soon, we were back at Pretty Corner Market, the street where Ashwini, Lej and I had been ambushed by Mahishasura and his two minions just a few days before. The exact spot where the tear had opened up was a little further ahead, on the balcony of a house at the end of the street. Like last time, the street was fairly busy. I could even see the old man with the cart of coconuts – he was OK!

Someone stepped away from a stall a few feet ahead, the glitter on her hair and skin sparkling in the sun. Chamundeshwari marched towards us. 'What do you think you are doing out here?' she demanded.

'I know I shouldn't be here,' I said quickly. 'It's not the cleverest thing I've ever done, but I had to—'

'It is unquestionably unwise,' she agreed, and Pip snorted a laugh. 'Even more unwise when you take into account the fact that you cannot get near that tear, Kiki. I know that is why you have come, and I told you already. That house and its balcony are heavily guarded.'

'But maybe we could distract the Asuras and—'

'I am *very* good at distractions,' Pip chimed in.

With a quick glance around us, Chamundeshwari put one hand on my shoulder and the other on Pip's and ushered us under the shelter of one of the larger stalls. Beautiful silk shawls lay across every surface of the stall, and I had to put my hands behind my back to stop myself from touching them.

'It is not possible,' Chamundeshwari said quietly.

I snapped my eyes away from a peacock-blue shawl and up to her face, realising suddenly that it couldn't possibly be a coincidence that she happened to be here this morning. 'You tried,' I said.

'I could not get past them, not even to catch a glimpse of the balcony and see if your possessions are still there.'

'You tried,' I said again, shocked.

She looked puzzled. 'I did tell you that if I could, I would.'

I put my arms around her waist and hugged her. She stood stock-still, obviously stunned, then very awkwardly patted me on the back.

'Do *I* get to be involved in this display of gratitude and affection?' Pip wanted to know.

I grabbed his sleeve and roped him into the hug, too, which only made Chamundeshwari even more awkward.

She extracted herself pretty quickly. 'Tell me this,' she said. 'Why does Brahma feel that the best way to defeat Mahishasura is to banish him? Why does Vishnu believe you should slay him instead?'

'I don't know,' I said. 'I never spoke to Brahma. He told Ashwini that I had to break the gandaberunda's eye. Maybe he knew I couldn't win any other way.'

'I do not believe that,' said Chamundeshwari, 'but I will respect his decision. That is what you should be doing right now, Kiki.'

'I know,' I said, ashamed. There was an entire Asura army searching the city for me, but I had come out anyway because my uncooperative, untrustworthy brain had drowned me in noise and anxiety and what-if this and what-if that until, in the end, I *had* to come out here to make it stop.

I should have just stayed put.

But if I could have, I would have.

Chamundeshwari tilted her head to one side. 'Tell me more about the gandaberunda,' she said. 'Brahma told your friend that breaking its eye would banish Mahishasura back to the Nowhere Place. How?'

'By turning this world back into ink and paper. When that happens, anyone here who came from other worlds will go back to where they came from.'

'But what—'

The sound of a terrible shriek cut her off.

Pip's face paled.

Shadows fell over the cobblestones of the street and there was another shriek from the sky. My heart went cold.

'They know you're here,' Chamundeshwari said. She stayed calm, but her eyes had narrowed. She pushed Pip and me out of the stall and into the street. 'Run! Quickly!'

I didn't dare look up. We bolted down Pretty Corner Market, but the shadows followed us. To my horror, there seemed to be more of them than there had been just seconds before.

We couldn't outrun them. Asuras materialised in front of us – some from the sky, some from the shade of the other streets. Chamundeshwari thrust Pip and me behind her, but they were all around us, all kinds of demon hybrids: bison, hawk, wolf, panther, creatures who were a mixture of different beasts, monsters who growled and snorted as they pressed in closer.

Chamundeshwari drew her sword and attacked. She moved like fire, fast and merciless and crackling with heat. Her sword flashed in a wide arc and three Asuras burst into smoke.

'Duck!' she shouted, and Pip and I dived for the ground as she pulled a shiny, viciously sharp steel disc out of her belt and threw it with one hand while keeping an enormous bison demon at bay with her sword.

The shiny disc, a chakra, spun in a circle. Everywhere it went, demons were destroyed in clouds of smoke.

Infuriated, the rest of the Asuras snarled and leapt at her. She was swarmed at once, but she was Chamundeshwari. They were nothing compared to her. They just kept coming, dozens of them, and the screech of steel was all I could hear, but she never faltered. She stood in front of us like a shield, the bravest warrior goddess in any world. They were no match for her.

Suddenly, I felt Pip torn away from me. I cried out as an enormous beaked Asura snatched him between its clawed feet and leapt into the air.

'Pip! *Pip!*'

'Kiki!'

I snatched at his foot, but it was whisked away as the Asura flapped its wings and went up, up, up. Chamundeshwari shouted at me, but I couldn't hear her over the sound of my heart pounding in my ears as I watched Pip get smaller and smaller.

And then a pair of enormous, powerful arms seized me around the waist. I screamed and struggled, but I was so small compared to the creature, little more than a doll shaken ruthlessly in the beast's grip.

Chamundeshwari spun around to reach for me, but she was too late. The Asura snatched me off the ground and flew into the sky.

18

There'd been a time when I would have thought that no experience in the world could be more incredible than soaring above my colourful city in the bluest of blue skies.

But, as a matter of fact, it was not at *all* fun.

This was possibly because I had my eyes squeezed shut and was screaming at the top of my voice.

Or, more likely, it was because I had been captured by a demon.

The most annoying thing about it was that, thanks to Ashwini, I knew exactly how to jab the Asura in the armpit to force her to let me go, but that skill was of absolutely no use to me right now. I was, frankly, safer in the painful grip of a monster than I would be plummeting out of the sky.

It seemed like for ever before I felt my feet slam into solid ground again. The Asura gave me a rough shake before letting me go and I immediately fell forward to my knees. I opened my eyes, nauseated and temporarily blinded by the light, and staggered to my feet.

I looked up at Lalith Mahal and gulped noisily.

'Move,' the Asura behind me growled. 'You're expected inside.'

'Where's Pip?'

'Move.'

She gave me a hard push. I jerked away and started walking. We were on a wide, long driveway, paved white and flanked by leering gargoyles carved out of ruby. Other Asuras slipped out from behind the gargoyles and came to watch me with malevolent, glittering eyes.

What had I done? If I had just stayed put like I was told to, none of this would have happened. If I had any control over my own brain, none of this would have happened. As I took one step after another towards the demon king's fortress, I had never felt more furious with myself. What if Pip was hurt? It would be all my fault.

Lalith Mahal was beautiful. It was wide rather than tall, and almost all white, with a handful of gold balconies and large, imposing doors the colour of apricots. Pure-white columns lined the front and a vast white dome crowned the top of the palace. I had drawn it almost exactly like the one in the real Mysore, at least on the outside.

White steps led from the drive up to an arch. I climbed the steps reluctantly, painfully aware of the hot, raspy breath of the demon behind me.

On the other side was a courtyard, sheltered by an enormous banyan tree. As we entered, I noticed something on the far side. Blackened wood, and what looked like burnt cloth.

My desk and curtains!

Mahishasura had them. But then why hadn't he used them? He had to know about the locator spell – why else would he bring some broken, tattered, ruined objects to his fortress? So why hadn't the Asuras come for me sooner? Had the Good Witch refused to perform the spell?

With an impatient grunt, the Asura grasped me by the back of my neck and forced me to move faster. We crossed the courtyard and stepped into one of the enormous rooms beyond. I tried to wriggle out of the Asura's grip (without poking her armpit and making her even crosser), but she held fast and pushed me across the room and into another. It was cool inside, out of the hot sun, and almost obnoxiously luxurious.

Then I started to notice little things that warped the beautiful picture. There were blank spaces on the walls where paintings of the old kings, queens and princesses had been torn down, claw marks across the handwoven tapestries and the faint, creepy smell of meat that had gone bad.

I didn't see Pip. Where was he? What had they done with him?

'This way,' growled the Asura.

She pushed me through a pair of arched doors guarded by two bison demons, and I found myself in an enormous room.

And there, on his throne, was Mahishasura.

I shuddered.

'Leave us,' he said in that deep, horrible voice.

The Asura obeyed immediately. She let go of my neck, bowed and retreated from the throne room. I didn't watch her go. I was alone with the demon king and I didn't dare take my eyes off him.

Mahishasura sat at ease on his beautiful golden throne, in a pose I must have drawn him in a dozen times, with his cruel amber eyes on me. In one hand, he held what looked like a collection of bones.

'They're carved out of marble,' he told me. He opened his fierce jaws and dropped the bones into his mouth. They crunched as he chewed, swallowed and licked his chops.

I clenched my hands tightly together to keep them from trembling. Mahishasura just watched me.

I swallowed. 'Where's Pip?'

'My Asuras tell me you think you can defeat me,' he said, as if I hadn't spoken. 'Is that true? *You*, who ran from me the last time we met?'

The amused tone of his voice made me feel small and cowardly. I gritted my teeth. 'You took this world from me. I *have* to defeat you.'

'Ah yes,' he said with a deep, cold chuckle. 'Of course you do.'

'My mother—'

'You and I both know this is not about your mother,' he cut me off, waving my words away. 'This is about you and it is about me. You said it yourself: you *have* to defeat me. Is that not why you created this world?'

'Why would I have created this world just to defeat you?' I asked, confused. 'I didn't know you were real. You were just a story to me.'

Mahishasura tossed his head and snorted air out of his nostrils. It took me a second to realise he was *laughing*. 'What an absurd, foolish child you are. Do you not see?'

'See what?'

'Do you think it was an accident that of all the stories you could have recreated, *mine* is the one you chose?'

I stared at him. Goosebumps spread over my skin, but I just clenched my hands tighter. 'I liked your story,' I said, my voice small and unsteady. 'That's all.'

He rose from the throne, his horns glinting in the light, and towered over me. '"That's all,"' he repeated, his voice little more than a low, mocking growl. 'Shall we remind ourselves of the story? There was once a perfect world, full of sunshine and joy. Then one day, there came a monster. And the world went dark.'

'I know the story,' I whispered.

'Then tell me why you chose it.'

My heart fluttered wildly, like a butterfly trying

frantically to escape a pair of cupped hands. I couldn't speak.

'There was a sunshine girl once, was there not?' said Mahishasura. His voice slithered into my mind, like a snake that finds its way into even the most hidden places. 'And then a monster took the sun away. So what did she do? She created a world in which a monster was defeated, hoping that would vanquish her own monster.'

'That ...' My throat was dry. 'That's not ...'

'No?' One clawed finger tapped my forehead, and I recoiled. 'Is there not a monster in there that you fear, Kiki Kallira?'

Tears filled my eyes. 'You don't know anything about me.'

'I know *everything* about you. I could not have broken into your world and taken it for my own if I didn't know you as well as I do.' He circled me, his hooves quiet as snow. 'You cannot vanquish me because I *am* you. I am the part of you that you fear most.'

'No! It's not true!'

'That is why you chose this story,' Mahishasura said. 'That is why you feel you *must* take this world back from me.'

'At the end of the story, you lost,' I found the nerve to say.

'Did I not come back? Am I not here now? That is what frightens you most, is it not? You fear that no matter what you do, the monsters will *always* be here.' He stepped closer, until I had to tilt my head right up to look into his wicked eyes. 'And they will,' he said. '*I* will.'

19

A bison demon pushed me into a cold, damp cell and slammed the heavy gate shut. I wrapped my arms around myself and shivered, watching the demon walk away.

'Kiki!'

I whirled around just in time for Pip to rush across the cell and slam into me, hugging me tightly. 'You're OK!' we both cried out at the same time.

'They put me in here a little while ago, but I didn't know what had happened to you,' Pip went on.

'They took me to Mahishasura first,' I said.

Pip's eyes went round. 'What did he say?'

'He ...' I couldn't say it.

I stepped back and huddled into myself. I wanted desperately not to think about what Mahishasura had said to me, so of course it was the *only* thing I could think about. Was he right? Had this world, this Mysore, just been a canvas on which I'd painted my messy, anxious brain? Maybe it had never only been a way to escape my own head, but had also been a way to take out the parts of me I hated and put them somewhere they could be beaten.

Mysore had been perfect before Mahishasura. I had been happy before my brain had turned on me. Had my version of Mahishasura always been just a cruel manifestation of whatever it was that made me lie awake at night worrying, and biting my nails until they were ragged, and having weird, terrible thoughts about unlocked front doors and murdered mothers?

Was *I* my own enemy?

The worst part, of course, was what he had said at the end. *I think you fear that no matter what you do, the monsters will always be here.*

Exhausted, I sat down on the floor of the cell and hugged my knees to my chest. All the noise in my head had given me a headache.

Then Pip, who settled down beside me, gave me a welcome distraction. 'By the way,' he said, with an awful lot of good cheer for someone in a demon king's cell, 'the Good Witch is over there.'

I followed the line of his finger to the cell right beside ours. A wall of bars separated the two, and, on the other side, I could see a young woman lying on her back on a thin cot and humming to herself.

'Hello,' I called.

She looked across at me. Her eyes were a bright purple, glittering like amethysts in a dark, pretty face crowned with long, thick dark hair. The set of her mouth and her hair reminded me of my mother.

'It's you,' she said. 'The whimsical architect of our world.'

I gave her a tiny smile. 'How long have you been here?'

'A thousand lives of a moon apple, a hundred turns of a golden goose and three flashes of sapphire,' she replied.

'And what is that in human time?' I asked tentatively.

She sighed, as if this was a very unreasonable request. 'Seven weeks.'

'That's the kind of thing she's said to pretty much every question I've asked her,' Pip told me. He paused, and reconsidered. 'Except for when I asked her if she could get us out of here using some kind of witchy witchery. She didn't answer that one at all.'

'Such foolery did not deserve a response,' said the Good Witch, her nose in the air. 'Would I still be here if I could get myself out?'

'I'm not sure her name suits her,' Pip said to me. 'The *Mean* Witch seems more like it.'

In spite of myself, I giggled.

'Where are the other prisoners?' I asked the Good Witch. 'Are you the only one?'

'They're in the land of stars and honey,' said the Good Witch. At my blank look, she rolled her eyes and translated: 'The other prisoners are dead. They're never here for long.'

'How did you make it to seven weeks?' Pip wanted to know.

'My witchy witchery, as you put it,' she said. 'He makes me cast spells for him every now and then.'

'Was one of those spells a locator spell on a burnt desk or ruined curtains?' I asked.

'It was not.'

So he hadn't asked her to find me. Why not?

'Now, if you don't mind,' the Good Witch went on,

'I am much too busy examining the insides of my eyelids to answer any more questions.'

So now was not a good time to ask her if she could help us get into Mysore Palace, then. Not that it mattered. We were all stuck here.

Hours passed. There were no windows in the cells, only dim lamps, so it was impossible to tell what time it was. Pip and I dozed on and off, waking in fits and starts.

'Why do you think we're still here?' Pip asked me at one point. 'I don't get it. They killed the other prisoners. Why keep us?'

Why *hadn't* Mahishasura and his Asuras just killed us instead of putting us here? I was the only person who could banish Mahishasura back to the Nowhere Place, after all, so it made sense to get rid of me as quickly as possible.

He wanted something from me. That was the only answer I could come up with.

But what?

Unless, of course, he was just doing what every wicked witch in every fairy tale did: he was going to fatten us up before he ate us.

Pip stretched and yawned, then promptly fell asleep with his head on my shoulder. I jostled him awake so that I could put my arm around him and let him cuddle up properly. 'Thank you for coming with me today,' I whispered. 'I'm so sorry I got you into this mess, but I'm glad you're here with me.'

'Me too,' he said, and started to snore.

I must have gone back to sleep, too, because the next thing I knew, I was startled awake by a loud clang as the cell door opened. A stag Asura loomed in the gap, two bowls in his cloven hands.

'Stew,' he grunted, plonking the bowls down.

Something grey sloshed inside the bowls. Pip made a face. 'Blech,' he said impolitely.

'That's your dinner, so eat it or you'll get nothing until breakfast,' the Asura growled, pointing his antlers at Pip in warning. He shut the cell door, turned a key noisily in the lock and loped away.

I *knew* they were trying to fatten us up.

'Kiki,' Pip whispered. 'I think he dropped the key.'

'That seems unlikely,' I said doubtfully.

Pip waited until the Asura's footsteps had completely faded before wriggling over to the cell door. He pushed his arm between two of the bars, as far as it would go, and scrabbled around the floor outside the door.

Then, with a look of pure delight, he pulled his arm back into the cell and opened his hand. There, on his palm, winked a set of keys.

I jumped up, incredulous. 'No way!'

'That has never happened before,' the Good Witch said, sitting bolt upright on her cot.

'I guess they've got careless,' Pip crowed. His glee was infectious. 'Come on. Let's get out of here!'

I hesitated. It *had* been careless. Maybe too careless? What if the Asura had dropped the keys on purpose? But why? Was it possible one of Mahishasura's minions actually wanted to help us?

What if it was a trap?

Or what if it really *had* just been an accident?

'Kiki.' Pip tugged at my arm. 'Come on.'

I had to stop this. We were only here because I kept overthinking things. I *had* to stop letting my anxiousness run away with me.

Once Pip had unlocked our cell door, I swallowed my uneasiness and followed him out. He let the Good Witch out, too.

'Can you cast any spells at all?' I asked the Good

Witch. It was one thing to get out of a cell. Quite another to get out of a fortress full of monsters.

'Two thousand and six, precisely,' she said loftily.

I scowled. 'And how many of those would help us get out of here?'

'Exactly zero,' she replied. 'The first spell Mahishasura got me to cast for him was one to prevent me from casting any others inside Lalith Mahal without his permission.'

So we would have to get out of here the old-fashioned way.

We crept away from the dark, damp cells and found ourselves at the top of a long flight of stone spiral stairs. We had to be in the enormous dome at the top of the palace. Cautiously, we took the stairs down to the bottom and then into a hallway. I kept expecting a hulking Asura guard to pounce from the dark, but there was no sign of any of them. The hallway led into a room, which led in turn to another hallway, but still, there was nobody.

Why wasn't anyone here?

Soon, we got to an arch that opened up on to the courtyard with the banyan tree that I'd seen earlier. It was dark and quiet this time, the shadows unnaturally long. Beyond the shelter of the banyan tree, between the branches, I could see the stars and the moon. That was all the light we had.

We hadn't seen a single Asura. There wasn't even any sign of the stag demon who had given us our stew and dropped the keys. Where had they all gone? They couldn't all be asleep, surely? Why was it so quiet?

The anxiousness was back, but it couldn't be helped. I was horribly troubled. And from the way her purple eyes searched the alcoves and shadows all around us, I could tell the Good Witch wasn't happy, either.

'That's the way out,' she murmured, pointing across the courtyard at the archway I had used to enter the palace.

Each step we took across the courtyard was agony. With each rustle of the banyan tree's leaves, with each shadow that flickered, I was sure we were done for. We had been so lucky. It couldn't possibly last.

But there was nothing. Just the wind, the dust and the moon.

Until the end.

We were just a few feet away from the archway when a shadow moved. This time, it wasn't a flicker.

This time, it slithered out of the dark and became the enormous horned creature in front of us.

The Good Witch froze. Pip reeled back, his eyes moving up, up, *up*.

Mahishasura laughed. 'Did you really think it would be so easy to escape me?'

'Did you know we were here the whole time?' Pip asked. His voice was a little squeaky, but it was a thousand times braver than I felt. 'Why didn't you stop us sooner?'

'Stop you? But that would have deprived me of the entertainment I've had watching you scurry around my fortress like frightened mice, jumping at every shadow.'

'That's unkind,' said Pip.

Mahishasura seemed to find this amusing, but he didn't spare Pip any more of his attention. His amber eyes glowed in the dark as they settled on me. 'Why do you still try?' he asked. 'You know now that to defeat me, you must also defeat yourself. You cannot win. I took this world from you and you could not stop me. I ruined your precious city and you could not stop me. I captured you and you could not stop me. So why, then, do you still try? You are just a weak little girl. What can you hope to do to me?'

I couldn't answer him. How could I? Everything he said was true.

But Pip was not silenced so easily. 'Ever since Kiki got here, you've hunted her. You've had your whole army out searching for a little girl. Why would you do that if you're so sure she can't hurt you?'

'Quiet,' growled the demon king.

'No,' said Pip defiantly. 'I want an answer. If Kiki has no power, why are you so afraid of her?'

I knew at once that it was the worst possible thing he could have said. Mahishasura let out a snarl that rattled me all the way down to my bones. The Good Witch covered her ears with her hands, but Pip didn't move. He stayed put, his chin up, eyes blazing.

One of Mahishasura's enormous hands closed around Pip's throat. He lifted him high and threw him across the courtyard like a rag doll.

There was a *crack*, and Pip went quiet for ever.

20

There was a scream, but the *whoosh* of blood roaring in my ears was so loud that it took me a moment to realise it had come from me. The shape of my scream was Pip's name, called out over and over, in the desperate hope that he would hear me and bounce up to his feet with that joyous grin and prove that somehow, impossibly, he was OK.

But Pip didn't move, or grin, or do any of the things that were so completely *Pip*. I ran to him and knelt beside him on the stone. 'Pip! Wake up! *Please* wake up!'

I didn't get an answer. I held his hands in mine and squeezed as hard as I could, but he felt so limp, so cold.

A shadow fell across Pip's face. I looked up into

Mahishasura's pitiless eyes. 'Why? He didn't do *anything* to you!'

'Why didn't you stop me?'

Each word hit my heart like a thousand sharp needles. I tried to speak, but nothing came out of my mouth.

'You didn't stop me because you couldn't,' he said ruthlessly. 'You could not save him. And you cannot save this world, either.'

I bent my head, wrapped my arms around Pip and sobbed. He had been my first friend, the made-up boy who came with me on hundreds of adventures, and now he was gone.

For a moment, that was all there was, just the grief and his soft, messy hair against my cheek, and then I felt a warm golden glow slide over my skin.

I looked up in confusion. The Good Witch was gone. With Mahishasura's attention on me, she had slipped out of the archway and down the steps. She wasn't inside Lalith Mahal any more.

She could use her power.

I clutched Pip tighter, terrified that we would be separated, but the golden glow wrapped itself around both of us, like a bubble; an orb of light in the dark night.

And then, suddenly, we weren't in the courtyard any more. We were in Crow House, right smack in the middle of the cosy front room, and there were startled shrieks from Suki and Jojo, who had been quietly minding their own business before we materialised out of thin air.

After that, it was chaos. The shrieks had the others rushing in, and a kaleidoscope of voices shouted 'Are you OK?' and 'We were so worried!' and 'Chamundeshwari said you'd both been captured, how did you get out?' and 'Who is *that*?'

Then Simha let out a roar, which silenced everyone immediately. The Good Witch cleared her throat. 'I am the Good Witch,' she said with a very dignified curtsy. 'We just escaped Lalith Mahal.'

'Kiki, you did it!' Suki said happily. 'You got her out!'

'Is Chamundeshwari OK?' I croaked. 'She was still fighting the Asuras when we were snatched away.'

'She hurt her shoulder, but she's all right,' Ashwini said. I felt her hand on my arm, squeezing affectionately, but I was still huddled over Pip and hadn't looked up. 'We were about to come and rescue you, but I have to admit I'm relieved we don't have to! I'm so glad you're both OK.'

'Kiki,' Lej said. I think it was the first time he had ever actually said my name. His voice was full of dread. 'Why are you holding Pip like that? Is he unconscious?'

'Come on,' Ashwini said gently. She put an arm around me and tugged me away from Pip. I let him go reluctantly, my heart cold. 'Let's see what's—'

And then all the colour drained out of her face and she stopped abruptly, her eyes fixed on Pip. Jojo sucked in a sharp breath. Suki let out a shrill cry.

Ashwini's lower lip wobbled. 'No,' she said. 'No, no, *no*. This isn't happening. This shouldn't have happened!'

Lej knelt on the rug beside Pip and searched frantically for a pulse. His eyes were wet. 'How?' he asked gruffly.

'The demon king threw him,' said the Good Witch.

Ashwini didn't reply immediately. She seemed to have lost all sense of reality. Her eyes were fixed on Pip and she just kept whispering, 'This shouldn't have happened' over and over. My heart went out to her. She was only thirteen years old and she had given everything to keep the Crows safe, but she hadn't been able to save Pip.

Because I had gone and got him killed.

Voices rose and fell around me, but I couldn't hear them. I sat back on my knees and bit my lip hard. All I could think about was how Pip had looked in his final moments, so much braver than I would ever be.

Then Simha offered to take Pip to Chamundeshwari, who would be able to make sure he was honoured and cremated. Ashwini was clearly unwilling to let him go, but she nodded and Simha left.

'Well,' said the Good Witch, 'I must go, too. Chikoo trees won't grow themselves.'

No one even tried to make sense of that, but Ashwini said, 'Wait.' Her voice cracked, but she pulled herself together and wiped away her tears. 'We still have to banish Mahishasura, now more than ever. Can you undo the protection spell on Mysore Palace?'

'The one that made the palace transform itself into a maze?' the Good Witch said. 'I am afraid I cannot. Kiki constructed the palace that way. No power of mine can undo anything she has done.'

There was a terrible silence. A fist closed around my heart and crushed. We had failed. *I* had failed.

'It was all for nothing,' Lej said.

'I am free,' said the Good Witch, a little

reproachfully. 'I don't call that *nothing*.' With an offended sniff, she vanished.

'Well done,' Suki said to Lej. 'Way to go and act like giving a person back their life is *nothing*. Pip wouldn't have taken kindly to that.'

Lej's cheeks coloured, but he turned to me and said harshly, 'It should have been you.'

I wiped tears off my cheek as the others protested. 'I know.'

'None of this would have happened if you had stayed put like you were supposed to,' he went on, his face full of pain and fury. 'What was so important that you *had* to go out there?'

'I couldn't stop myself,' was all I could say. 'I know I shouldn't have gone. I know that. This is my fault. I *know* that.'

'Stop it,' Jojo said to Lej, his hands clenched on the arms of his chair. 'None of this will bring Pip back. All we can do now is look after each other.'

'And make Mahishasura sorry for what he's done,' Suki added, her brown eyes flashing.

Lej shot a furious look my way. 'How? *She* was supposed to be the answer, but it turns out she's no help at all. I told you,' he added, turning his glare on

Ashwini this time, 'I *told* you she was more likely to get us killed than fix anything!'

There was a tense pause, and then Ashwini said softly, 'Maybe you should go upstairs, Kiki. You don't have to listen to this.'

And my being there was making things worse. It was kind of her not to say it, but it was true. This was *their* home and *their* family. I was just an intruder on their grief.

I left the room quietly. Halfway up the stairs, I couldn't keep the tears away any more, so I bit my lip and cried as quietly as I could. Inside my room, I sat on the floor, my back pushing the door closed, and buried my face in my arms.

A tiny tyrant. It was what Lej had called me last night, right before I had left Crow House just to get some measure of control over my own mind. *A tiny tyrant.* A petulant child.

Maybe that was all I was. Maybe everything I had ever done had been about stamping my foot and throwing a tantrum because I had no power over myself, let alone over anything else. I wasn't the master of my fate. I wasn't the captain of my soul.

I hadn't been able to stop Mahishasura from taking

over the world I created. I hadn't been able to keep Pip safe.

I hadn't been able to stop my own mind from turning on me.

I pushed myself off the door and crumpled into the bed. The rainbow unicorns on my pyjamas sparkled in the moonlight, but for once the colours didn't cheer me up. I wished I was home with Mum. I wanted the boring, normal things again: eating cake while Mum and I watched TV, feeding ducks in the park with Emily, reading books, pulling out a pencil and drawing any old thing that happened to catch my attention. I wanted my mother to make me feel better. I wanted to go home.

I used the back of one hand to scrub the tears off my face, then pulled my pencil out of my pocket. There was paper on the other side of the room, but I pressed the pencil to the white surface of the windowsill. The first marks were random, but then I pressed harder because the fist squeezing my heart needed something else to crush.

Art had saved me before. Maybe it could save me now.

Why couldn't it have saved Pip?

A small bird took shape on the windowsill, quick strokes of wings and beak and bright eyes. I pressed harder. A pair of tiny feet.

The pencil broke with a loud snap.

And the bird shook itself free of the windowsill and flew out into the warm, silver night.

21

Astonished, I gawked into the night until the little white bird vanished over the rooftops of Mysore. Then I looked down at the windowsill, where the painted-white wood had been smooth and where now the two halves of my pencil lay in a bird-shaped dip.

Had I just *sketched* a bird to life? Yes, I was in a pocket universe that had been created out of my sketchbook, so you would think that nothing could possibly surprise me any more, but this was a whole new level of weirdness. Mahishasura's power had brought my sketchbook to life, and I had just about wrapped my head around that, but this? This was me.

I picked up the half of the pencil with the nib still intact, but my hand trembled. A part of me wanted to try drawing another picture, just to find out if everything I drew here would become real, but a bigger part of me was terrified. I couldn't trust myself. This world was already full of my monsters. Pip had been *killed* by one of those monsters.

I had broken too many things already.

I tucked the pencil piece back into my pocket. The fist around my heart squeezed tighter.

There was a soft knock at the door. It was Ashwini. Her eyes were red and her face was swollen from crying, but she looked calm. She shut the door and sat quietly beside me on my bed. 'I'm sorry about what happened downstairs,' she said. 'Lej wasn't fair to you.'

'He was right,' I said.

'You knew Pip,' she said with a small smile. 'I'm going to assume he followed you when you left, didn't he? He did that because he wanted to, because he was a good friend. You didn't make him do it. You're not responsible for his death.'

I clenched my hands together. I was still freaked out after the bird, and I wanted to tell Ashwini about it just so someone could help me make sense of it, but now wasn't the time. She needed me to be her friend right now.

'How are you?' I asked softly.

She forced a smile. 'I'm OK. This is just like everything else. You get past it by taking one step, and then another, and then another.'

'You don't have to put on a brave face for me,' I said. 'You don't have to pretend you're OK.'

For a moment, her lower lip trembled and it looked like she might break down, but I watched her clench her jaw and brush her tears aside. 'I'm fine.'

'OK,' I said gently. I wasn't going to force her to talk about it.

She was quiet for a few minutes, but then she said, 'Will you tell me what happened in Lalith Mahal?'

I nodded. She probably wanted to know what Pip had done in the last few hours of his life, and I owed her that. So I told her the whole story. All of it. Even the part in the throne room.

When I was finished, she said, 'You know it's not true, don't you?'

'What's not true?'

'That there's something wrong with you. It's not true.' I started to shake my head, but she shook hers harder and said firmly, 'It's *not* true.'

'Whatever this is, I hate it,' I burst out. 'The day I created this world, my mind got stuck on one thing and wouldn't leave me alone and the only way to make it stop was to come home and check my front door. Today, it did the same thing and the only way to make it stop was to go back to the tear between worlds. And look what happened!'

'Kiki ...'

'I feel like I can't breathe because it's so crowded inside my head. And I can't make it stop. I never know when it's going to happen. I don't trust myself when it happens. I can't trust my own brain.'

'But, Kiki, none of that means there's something wrong with you,' she insisted. 'It's just an illness.'

I stilled. 'What?'

'An illness,' she said. 'A chronic condition. You know?'

I blinked. 'That's all? Just an illness?'

'That's all,' she said. 'I don't know much, but I do know that sometimes our brains can get ill, not just our bodies. You must know that, too, right?'

'Yes, but ...' I trailed off. Was it possible?

'Well, there you go. I reckon that's all this is. It's something that's a part of you, but it's not all of you.'

I swallowed. 'It never occurred to me to think of it that way. I guess it was easier to think of it as some kind of monster that moved into my brain and ruined it, but it's not, is it? I just wish I wasn't quite so weak and wimpy. Maybe I'd be able to get better, then.'

She snorted. 'Do you think Jojo is weak and wimpy because he can't walk?'

'No, of course not,' I said, surprised. 'What does him not being able to walk have to do with it?'

She rolled her eyes. 'Your brain is to you what his legs are to him, silly. Neither works exactly the way you expect them to, but that doesn't make either of you weak or wimpy or *lesser* than anyone else.'

There was a feeling inside me that was so big and so powerful that I didn't know what to call it. The best I could do was this: I felt like I'd been taken apart and put back together again.

Maybe, just maybe, my brain wasn't some kind of monstrous thing I couldn't trust. It was just a little different.

Mahishasura's voice came back to me. *I think you fear that no matter what you do, the monsters will always be here.*

'Do you think I'll always feel like this?' I asked quietly.

'Maybe,' said Ashwini. 'Maybe not. But if you do,

I suspect that over time, you'll find ways to make it less of a pain in the butt, like how Jojo's wheelchair helps him. Maybe there's something a doctor can do to help you, too?' She smiled at the stunned expression on my face, and for the first time since she had seen Pip downstairs, the twinkle in her eye was back. 'Wow, you really didn't consider any of this, did you?'

'I was just so *angry* with myself,' I said. 'I was so sure there was something wrong with me and it was all my fault. I never even told Mum how bad it was. She would probably have made me feel a lot better if I had.'

'And do you feel better now?'

'*Yes*,' I said. I knew it wouldn't be easy to shake away all the shame and guilt and anger that I'd let settle inside me, but just knowing that I didn't have to be afraid of myself any more made such a difference.

I threw my arms around Ashwini and hugged her. 'Thank you,' I said, almost in tears again. I looked into her pointy pixie face. 'You're much too wise to be thirteen, you know.'

Her smile faltered. 'Well, that's thanks to you,' she said. 'I guess you had to make me all grown-up and smart to be able to look after everyone else, right?'

I searched her face anxiously. 'Are you *sure* you're OK? I know I kind of took over the conversation for a few minutes there, but I'm here if you want to talk about Pip.'

'Actually, it was nice not to think of everything else for a while,' she said. 'So I should thank *you* for distracting me.' She stood up. 'I should check on the others. The twins are supposed to be in bed, but I'm sure they're still awake. Oh, by the way,' she added, 'we'll be taking Pip's ashes to the Kaveri tomorrow. We'll go after dark, when we're less likely to be spotted. You should come with us.'

She didn't mention Mahishasura, and I didn't ask. After all, what could either of us say? The Good Witch couldn't help us. Mysore Palace was still impassable. And Mahishasura was too strong to fight.

How were we supposed to win?

22

Exhausted, I staggered in and out of a shower, put my poor unicorn pyjamas into another cycle in the wash (minus my pencil this time), and collapsed into a dreamless sleep. When Suki woke me, the sun was blazing hot and I had been asleep in the full glare of it for so long that my shoulder was sunburnt. Awesome.

I tried not to think of how much I hated that it had been Suki who had come to wake me instead of Pip.

'Simha made lunch,' Suki said, and winced dramatically. 'I think it would be rude not to eat it, but I am not convinced that lions are good cooks.'

That got my attention. 'What did he make?'

'Um. Rabbit.'

'Rabbit,' I repeated.

'Yep. He went out this morning, hunted a rabbit, stuck it in the oven and put it on the table. There's more.' Suki took a deep breath. 'He didn't use any spices.'

'He wants us to eat *bland* rabbit?'

'He told us we could flavour it with tea like he does,' said Suki.

This was too much for me. 'I think I'll stay up here, thanks.'

She giggled, then clapped a hand over her mouth like she was shocked she had done such a thing. I followed her downstairs, reluctantly.

There was an atmosphere of doom in the kitchen, with everyone eyeing the crispy rabbit on the table with deep suspicion. Simha hovered close by, clearly excited to see us eat the fruits of his labours. When his back was turned, Jojo's hand crept towards the salt, but Samara smacked it away so he wouldn't hurt Simha's feelings. At which point there was really nothing to do except eat the rabbit.

For a few minutes, as grimaces were covertly swapped around the table and cries of 'Yummy!' were forced out through pained smiles, it felt like Pip was still here, there were no Asuras and nothing had ever gone wrong. Even Lej made his way gamely through his portion of the rabbit, and, in the end, the look of pride on Simha's face when he saw our empty plates made it all worth it.

My hand closed over the pencil stub in my pocket. I wanted so badly to draw them all just like this. Taking one step, and another, and another, in spite of how much they had been hurt.

After lunch, much to everyone's horror, Simha informed us that what we needed after losing Pip was, and I quote, *some nurturing*. Having apparently decided that that nurturing should fall to him, he embarked on cleaning the house, a process that involved licking dust off the surfaces and surfing down the halls on soapy dishcloths. Then he made a menu of meals he planned to cook over the next week, and Suki, who sneaked up behind him to read his very awkward writing, raced back to report that she had spotted alarming phrases like *salt is unhealthy* and *absolutely no sugar*.

'This cannot stand,' she wailed. 'What are we supposed to do without cake?'

'Are *you* going to tell the lion he can't cook for us any more?' Lej demanded. 'Have you seen the size of his teeth?'

Later, as planned, we slipped across the city to the river after dark. The Kaveri shimmered like liquid silver in the full light of the moon, and the forest on the other side of the river whispered and hummed in the wind. We stood quietly on a bridge that arched across the river and scattered Pip's ashes over the water.

As we walked away, I looked back one last time. And for just one moment, I could have sworn I saw a crow taking flight into the night.

23

I woke to thunder. Startling awake, I looked out of the window, into the pinkish predawn. Dark grey clouds rolled across the sky, seething and furious, and thunder crashed over the city. I covered my ears. I had never heard thunder this loud. And why wasn't there any rain?

The skies roared and an enormous bolt of lightning struck the top of the Chamundi Hills. Then another struck one of the jewel-bright houses in the city, making the earth tremble. The thunder crashed again.

My door slammed open, making me jump, and Ashwini burst in. 'Come on,' she said, shouting over the sound of the thunder. 'We have to go!'

'Go where?'

'To the gandaberunda,' she said.

Dread made my stomach lurch. 'The thunder, the lightning,' I said. 'It's not just a storm, is it? It's Mahishasura.'

'He's trying to use what little power he has to rip open the tear between worlds even wider,' she said. Her eyes were wide and frantic, her entire body jittery. 'This is what happened when the tear opened up the first time. I don't know if he *can* tear it any wider, but we can't take that chance. If we want to stop him, we have to break that statue's eye *now*!'

'But we still don't know how to get to it!'

'I've got ropes downstairs. We'll climb the walls of the palace.'

'That's a *terrible* idea! You said there are Asuras circling the statue and guarding it at all times. They'll see us and stop us in no time.'

'Nope,' she said, practically bouncing off the walls. 'Not right now. Not with *that* storm in the sky. Come *on*, Kiki. I'll wait for you downstairs.'

'What about the others?' I asked, as I shoved my feet into Pip's shoes.

Her face was grim. 'I made them all promise to stay here. I can't lose anyone else. I wouldn't even have come to get *you* if you weren't the only one who can break the eye.'

She darted out, and it occurred to me that if we did this, if we succeeded, this would be the last time I would ever be in this house.

No, I couldn't think about that. There was too much grief already, I couldn't start thinking about how much I would miss everyone else.

Instead, I went to Pip's room and grabbed one of his old satchels. I filled it with whatever I could think of that might come in handy, both from his room and mine, and then I ran down the stairs before I could chicken out.

I didn't see any of the others on my way down. It was probably for the best; I didn't know if I could bear to say goodbye.

In the front hallway, Ashwini strapped her sword to her back and grabbed a tightly coiled rope.

'Wait,' I said. 'Put this on.'

I handed her a long, darkish-brown jacket, just like the one I'd put on before leaving my room. They were pretty ugly, but that didn't matter as much as what they were made of. I had helped Jojo sew stardust into them.

'Glamour jackets,' I said, when Ashwini looked confused. 'They'll make it difficult for any Asuras out there to see us. Jojo says their eyes should slide right past us.'

'Huh,' she said proudly. 'Good thinking.'

I followed her out of the front door, my stomach churning. I didn't like this. In fact, I was terrified and I hated every part of it, but as the thunder crashed and rolled above us, I knew I had no choice. I had to do this. I couldn't fail. Not this time.

Mysore was a ghost town as we ran across the square. Ashwini led the way, darting this way and that, never faltering in spite of the mist, the shadows and the flashes of lightning. I didn't know for sure if our glamour jackets were working or not, but the handful of Asuras we spotted prowling the streets didn't come near us, so I liked to think Jojo's work had done the trick.

High in the sky, my pastel castle was surrounded by thunder and electricity. I expected it to catch fire, shatter or fall, but it didn't. It was my whimsical, silly castle; the last piece of the whimsical sunshine girl I had once been, and it looked like it would survive. So would she. Girl and castle would both outlast the storm.

'There!' Ashwini shouted over the roar of the thunder.

Up ahead were the open gates of Mysore Palace, bent and creaking in the wind. I could see all the way down the brick drive, past the ashoka trees and mulberry bushes, to the great domes of the palace. I could even see the silhouette of the gandaberunda, dark against the flashing sky.

But there was a problem: two Asuras stood at the gates, their hulking forms looming across the opening. I couldn't see much beyond their four-legged silhouettes, but I could definitely see sharp teeth in strong, canine muzzles.

'I don't think the glamour jackets will get us past *them*,' I whispered, ducking back behind the line of houses we'd followed up to the palace. 'We'd have to squeeze past them and I think they'd notice that.'

'It wouldn't matter,' said Ashwini. 'They're wolf Asuras. Mahishasura likes to use wolves as guards because they have the best noses. Glamour or no glamour, they'd smell us if we got close.'

But my heart leapt. 'Did you say *wolf* Asuras?'

'Yes,' she said, frowning. 'You can tell by the shape

of the head and the four legs. Stay here. I should be able to get them both out of the way.'

I grabbed her arm before she could pull her sword off her back. 'No,' I said quickly. 'If you fight them, others might see. It'll attract too much attention.'

Ashwini looked bewildered. 'But how else are we to get to the palace?'

'There was once a little girl,' I said, with the kind of mischief Pip would have been proud of, 'and she met a wolf in a deep dark forest.'

Her eyes widened. 'You're not going to ...'

I pulled an apple out of Pip's satchel and took a bite.

The instant my teeth broke the skin of the ripe fruit, both Asuras snapped their heads in our direction. Their muzzles snapped and their eyes flashed yellow. Even though Samara had told me wolves couldn't resist the scent of apple juice, it was frankly terrifying to actually see it in action.

I threw the fruit down the line of houses, as far away from the palace as I could.

Silent, breathless, Ashwini and I watched as the wolves wrestled with themselves, trembling from the effort of not following the scent of the fruit. 'We cannot,' one growled to the other. 'We must not.'

'It would only take a moment or two to find it,' the other argued. 'What would be the harm?'

They hesitated for a split second, and then one broke rank, bolting in the direction I'd thrown the apple. The other snarled, realising he was about to miss out, and ran after the first.

'You know,' Ashwini said, sputtering a laugh, 'when Samara first told me that story, I was pretty sure she'd made it up. I owe her an apology.' She shook her head. 'I can't believe you packed an *apple.*'

'I packed two, thank you very much!'

With our way temporarily cleared, we raced across the wide street to the palace gates and ran down the brick drive, heedless of the thorns in the overgrowth. We stopped at the arch over the palace entrance, where the last time we'd been here, the porch had crumbled into an endless ravine and had almost taken Lej with it. The impassable darkness between us and the doors felt like a taunt.

I felt Ashwini take my hand and squeeze. 'We can do this,' she said. 'We *need* to do this.'

She approached one of the tall columns that lined

the front of the palace and started to unwind the coil of rope. 'I figure if we can loop the rope over the spikes of that balcony, we can use it to climb up this column. And then we—'

'Do you hear that?' I asked.

She paused, turning back. I hadn't moved. I could hear *something*.

'I can't hear anything over the storm,' she said. 'Come on, I need your help with these ropes.'

It was a whisper. It seemed extremely unlikely that I could hear a whisper over the roar of the thunder, but I could.

'Kiki.'

'Who is that?' I jerked, pressing a hand to my ear. 'Who are you?'

'You know who I am.'

And as I looked up at the doors ahead of me, the domes above me, the palace that seemed to reach for me, I did know.

'You're the palace,' I breathed in wonder.

'Yes.'

Ashwini was staring at me, baffled, and I could only guess how weird I looked standing there apparently talking to myself.

'Why didn't you speak to me when I was here before?' I asked the palace.

'*You were not ready to listen.*'

Great. A cryptic palace.

'*Ropes and tools will not get you to the gandaberunda,*' the palace went on. '*Only you can do that.*'

'So I can come in? You'll show me the way?'

'*You do not need me to do that. You are enough.*'

I was pretty sure that wasn't true, but there was something about the palace's voice in my ear, the sense of welcome, that made me feel like I had to find out one way or another.

'Leave the ropes,' I said to Ashwini. 'The palace thinks I can get us past its traps.'

Ashwini took this in her stride. 'OK then,' she said, dropping the ropes and coming back to my side. 'Let's go.'

Suddenly, I remembered one of the first things she had ever told me, back in London. *You have more power over that world than even Mahishasura does.* I had let myself forget that. I had spent so long convinced that I was helpless, that I was weaker than the monsters, that I'd had both my world and my mind stolen from me,

I hadn't considered that maybe none of that was true. Maybe I had more power than I had ever realised.

'The only other way into the palace is the botanical garden,' I said.

'The maze you said you couldn't get past last time?'

I took a deep breath. 'I think I can now.'

So, with thunder crashing above us, we skirted the edge of the palace and slipped around the eastern side, to the tall, overgrown hedges that surrounded the botanical garden. There was a rusty unlocked gate tucked into the corner of a hedge. I pushed it open and we stepped into the maze.

At first, nothing about it seemed unusual. Like just about every outdoor maze ever, the shrubs and trees were tall and dense, forming walls on either side of us. Glowing flowers and sparkling leaves were sprinkled across the dark green foliage, and tiny twinkling fireflies danced around us (or were they fairies? I definitely remembered drawing fairies in my sketchbook!).

But as we walked carefully down the only path available, our feet crunching on the dry leaves underneath, there was a rustling all around us ... and the hedges *moved*. Ashwini jumped backwards as shrubs slid in front of her, closing off the path ahead.

'I guess we have to find a different way,' she said, eyes wide.

We retraced our steps until we found a small gap in the hedges that hadn't been there before. On the other side was a fork, two paths leading in opposite directions, both turning sharp corners around tall, thick trees so that we couldn't see where they led.

'Which way?' Ashwini asked me.

'It doesn't matter,' I said. 'The maze will keep moving, closing off our paths and opening new ones. It'll never stay still.'

'Then how are we supposed to find a way out of it?'

'You'll see,' I said, my whole body tight with dread.

'Kiki,' said Ashwini, with certain doom in her voice. 'What have you done?'

'I wanted to make it scary. So I added stuff I was scared of.'

She looked up at the sky, probably to implore the universe to explain why I had been foisted upon her.

As we picked our way through the maze, backtracking each time our paths were blocked, my nerves felt more and more frayed, the dread unbearable.

It was almost a relief when it finally happened,

when we heard the clicking, skittering sounds ahead of us.

'*That* is how we get out,' I said, gulping nervously.

They spilt out of the hedges and trees, swarming the path, dozens and dozens of them, each the size of a small cat, all of them clicking and skittering and fixing their beady black eyes on us.

'Mechanical spiders?' Ashwini demanded, appalled. 'Are you *kidding* me?'

'I'm sorry!'

'So the maze will let us out if we – what? Defeat this army of hideous oversized spiders?'

I couldn't take my eyes off the awful creatures, but I nodded. How had I ever found a tiny spider in the corner of my bedroom frightening? That was *nothing* compared to this horror I had created for myself!

But, unexpectedly, Ashwini perked up. 'Well,' she said, 'at least I get to use my sword now.'

With a screech of steel, she pulled her sword off her back and leapt into the seething mass of mechanical spiders. She hacked away at the army, sending spiders flying into the trees and splitting the air with the shriek of metal parts breaking apart.

As she knocked them back a few at a time, I saw the wall of trees up ahead part in half, leaving us an opening beyond the spiders.

'I can hold them off,' she shouted, spotting it, too. 'Run!'

Every part of me wanted to run. I could probably jump over the spiders and race for the exit while she held them back. There were so many of them, and several of them had peeled away from Ashwini and were coming towards me, and I didn't have a sword or bow or even a stick with which to keep them at bay.

But I'd run away and left her behind once before. I wasn't going to do it again.

So I dropped my satchel to the ground and knelt beside it, scrabbling frantically inside. Where was it? Where was it?

'Kiki!' Ashwini yelled. *'Go!'*

Where had I put it? I knew I'd packed it!

The horrible *clickety-click* sounds grew louder. They were coming, they were almost on me—

My hand closed over a bottle.

'Get back!' I shouted.

Ashwini jerked around, hesitated, and then leapt

back, just as I uncorked the bottle and threw it at the army of spiders.

The bottle smashed as soon as it hit metal, and Suki's freezing potion splashed all over the spiders. Drops sprayed everywhere, narrowly missing us, catching all but the spiders right at our feet. Ashwini slashed at them, I kicked one into the hedge, and when we both looked up, the rest of the spiders had gone completely still.

'*Creative*,' said the voice of the palace in my ear. '*I like it.*'

'It'll wear off soon,' I said, trying to catch my breath. My heart was so loud, I could barely hear anything else. 'We should get out of here while we can.'

We stepped carefully around frozen mechanical legs. As we crossed the last few feet of the maze and pushed open a pair of glass doors, I could feel Ashwini watching me.

'Why didn't you just go?' she asked.

'It's like you said,' I told her. 'I'm not losing anyone else.'

24

We stepped through the doors into a ballroom. It was enormous, and, like Lalith Mahal, it was richly decorated, with glorious tapestries on the walls, luxurious armchairs around the sides of the room and a smooth wooden floor that must have once been brightly polished, but was now dusty and dull.

Three different doors led out of the ballroom. I searched my memories for all the sketches and maps I'd made of the palace. 'I think that door leads to the summer parlour, and that one to the ground floor of the library,' I said, pointing left and then right. 'Which means the third door should take us out to the entrance hall and the stairs.'

There were more tapestries, paintings and beautiful, thick rugs in the entrance hall. A grand flight of white marble stairs led up to the next floor, flanked by gold bannisters. But there were dead leaves, dust and cobwebs everywhere, which made the opulent palace feel sad and eerie.

At the top of the first flight of stairs, Ashwini looked around for the next one. 'This is where the hiding staircases are,' I said. 'We'll have to go looking for them.'

'Of course we will,' she sighed. 'It would have been too easy otherwise. Boring, even. Me, I *like* to set my life to maximum-difficulty mode. It's so much more fun that way!'

'Are you going to help me look, or are you going to keep treating me to your delightful gift for sarcasm?'

'Can't I do both?'

I smothered a laugh and started down the cream-coloured carpeted hallway. The second floor of the palace had a number of rich, elegant rooms: another library level, an art gallery, the royal family's private dining room and several guest suites. Somewhere between the dusty, ancient books and the four-poster beds draped with cobwebs, we found the first flight of stairs.

'The first?' Ashwini repeated. 'What do you mean, the *first*?'

'There are two hiding staircases. They lead to different places.' I was about to look for the other one when I heard her footsteps clatter up the staircase. I spun around. 'Wait! You don't know where that's going to end up!'

I raced after her. The stairs were steep and narrow, positioned in the middle of the room with a door at the top that seemed to lead nowhere. Ashwini turned the doorknob, and when the door opened, in spite of the fact that the door was hovering by itself in mid-air, I could see the cosy lavender walls and white panels of a room on the other side.

Panic seized me. I grabbed hold of Ashwini's arm, hauling her back before she could step over the threshold into the room. The momentum nearly sent us both tumbling back down the stairs.

'Kiki!' she protested.

I slammed the door shut. 'This is the wrong staircase. That room? That was the Room with No Doors.'

'I just saw a door!'

'And if you'd stepped into the room, that door would have sealed shut and vanished.'

Ashwini blinked. 'Are you telling me that if

someone were to accidentally get themselves stuck in that room, they'd have no way out?'

'Pretty much.' I stomped back down the staircase. 'You were almost stuck in there for ever.'

Just like Lej had almost fallen down a dark chasm right outside the palace.

There was a pause. Ashwini must have seen something on my face, because hers softened and she said very gently, 'Almost, Kiki. I was *almost* stuck in there for ever. You're the reason I'm not.' And then, as if she was surprised, she added, 'You *do* know what you're doing.'

Did I know what I was doing?

But as soon as that question crossed my mind, I knew the answer. I had kept Lej from falling. I had stopped Ashwini before she'd stepped over the threshold.

I had laid these traps. I knew how to beat them.

'*You see?*' said the palace. '*You know the way. You just got lost for a little while.*'

For the first time in days, I didn't feel like I was hopelessly out of my depth. For the first time in a long, long while, I wasn't afraid or uncertain. I could do this.

I reached for a loose rainbow thread at the cuff of my pyjamas and tore it free. I tied it around the bottom post of the staircase's white iron handrail.

'What's that for?' Ashwini asked.

'So that we know this is the wrong staircase next time we see it.'

She realised why this was necessary as soon as she got off the staircase. The moment her feet touched the solid floor, the staircase literally zoomed across the room and out the door to find a new hiding place.

We found it twice more before we finally stumbled across a staircase without the bright thread knotted around the bottom post. It led us safely to the third floor of the palace, where we found the music room, the observatory, the royal family's bedrooms, the nursery and the playroom.

'We have to go in here,' I said, pausing at the door of the playroom. 'There's a key we need if we want to get past the next floor. So, um, try not to scream.'

'I fight Asuras every day, Kiki,' Ashwini said, affronted. 'I just faced down an army of horrid mechanical spiders. I am *not* going to scream.'

She marched past me into the playroom—

And screamed her head off.

'Why?' she wailed. '*Why* would you do this?'

I felt my cheeks go pink. 'It wasn't supposed to be creepy.'

'HOW CAN THIS NOT BE CREEPY?'

I could kind of see her point because, well, the toys in the playroom had come alive.

Not all of them. Just the dolls.

Maybe that made it worse.

Three porcelain dolls sat around a little table, with pastel-painted wooden cakes and a fluffy teapot in front of them. One was pouring pretend-tea out of the pot, while another was nibbling on a pretend-cake.

The third turned her head and blinked glassy green eyes at me. 'Would you like some tea?' she asked, in a sweet, musical voice.

Ashwini clamped a hand over her eyes. 'I cannot,' she moaned. 'I one hundred per cent cannot.'

'We have to,' I hissed. 'If they like us, they'll give us the key.'

Shuddering, and with enormous reluctance, Ashwini followed me to the table. The empty chairs were far too small for us, so I moved them aside and we knelt in the gaps.

The green-eyed doll smiled, tilting her little head

to one side. 'Tell me,' she said, as polite as a princess, 'what is *your* favourite tea?'

'Um,' I said, sure there were wrong answers. 'Peppermint?'

With a *snick* of porcelain rubbing against porcelain, the second doll turned her head to me. 'Peppermint,' she repeated, her hand closing tight over the knife meant for cutting the cake.

Uh-oh.

'Peppermint *and* ginger,' I said, and copied the first doll's sweet, excessively polite tone. 'The *only* tea fit for a princess.'

Slightly mollified, the second doll nodded, her nose in the air.

She did not let go of the knife.

I was pretty sure we stood no chance, considering at least one of the dolls didn't like me and Ashwini displayed all the charm of an unconscious moose over the course of the tea party, but somehow, miraculously, the green-eyed doll gave me a graceful curtsy when it was over and dropped a silver key into my hand.

'Give me mechanical spiders any day,' Ashwini declared, practically knocking me over in her haste to get out of the playroom. 'Any. Day.'

From there, it was a (thankfully uncomplicated!) flight of stairs directly up into a vast circular room with nine locked doors leading out of it. My heart felt heavy with dread.

'Let me guess,' said my snarky not-ancestor. 'This is the Room with Many Doors?'

'Yep.'

'And what terrible catastrophe will befall us if we try the silver key in the wrong door?'

'The key will dissolve.'

'Which will force us to go back downstairs and relive the tea party horror to get a new key,' Ashwini guessed, closing her eyes as if in acute pain. 'Kiki, I haven't asked you for much—'

'You asked me to banish a demon king!'

'—but I am *begging* you now to pick the right door. I refuse to go back down there and face those porcelain nightmares again.'

'Well, you're in luck,' I said, 'because I lied. I only said that because I didn't want to scare you, but I think you'll actually prefer this to the dolls. If we pick the wrong door, the key will be fine.' I gestured upwards. 'But *that* will eat us.'

Ashwini's eyes snapped up to the ceiling. They

went wide, and her hand inched towards the sword on her back. And I knew I'd regret it, but I looked, too.

Defying all laws of gravity, an enormous white serpent lay coiled against the ceiling, scales glinting in the artificial moonlight. It was silent and still, apart from two cold silver eyes that blinked slowly at us.

'I think I *do* prefer this to the dolls,' Ashwini remarked. 'But I, for one, am not interested in being eaten. So I'll just get my sword and—'

As soon as her hand got within an inch of the hilt, the serpent on the ceiling hissed, fangs flashing in warning.

'OK,' she said, lowering her hand. 'We'll pick a door first. Is there some trick to figuring out which is the right one? They all look identical to me.'

Think, Kiki. What could I do? How could I narrow down the right door when there were nine to choose from and a giant serpent was waiting to devour us?

Was there something I'd packed in Pip's satchel that could help? I didn't think the other apple would work as well on a serpent as it had on the wolf Asuras, but maybe there was something else—

Wait!

Heart pounding fiercely in my chest, I reached into Pip's satchel and seized the small round ball tucked deep into the back pocket.

Ashwini went a little pale. 'Is that ...'

'You might want to hold your breath,' I said, and released one of Pip's many stink bombs into the room.

As soon as the hideous, vile stench escaped from the ball and hit the air, the serpent reared back, its slit nostrils flaring in revulsion. Beside me, Ashwini gagged, and I was pretty sure I was about to be sick, but the serpent was absolutely horrified.

And, as I'd hoped, the first thing it did was look for a way out.

'There!' I gasped between clenched teeth, as the serpent lunged towards a door on the far north of the room. 'That one!'

We rushed to the door. We'd picked the right one, so all the serpent could do was hiss furiously, bound by the rules. I fumbled with the silver key, the stink so overpowering that I could barely keep my hands steady, and turned it in the lock.

There was a *click*, the door swung open and one final flight of stairs loomed ahead of us.

We ran.

The door crashed shut, cutting us off from both serpent and stink.

'*Arghafffargh*,' Ashwini sputtered, smacking at herself as if that would knock away any last traces of the stink bomb.

I stepped off the stairs and let my breath out in a rush, pretty much ready to collapse on the thick cream-coloured carpet of the open, airy hallway ahead.

We'd done it. *I'd* done it.

Once she'd recovered, Ashwini asked with foreboding, 'What's next?'

'This is the top floor,' I said, as my knees wobbled. 'The gandaberunda is next.'

25

At the end of the hallway, right below the highest dome of
the palace, we pushed open a window and stepped out
on to a delicate balcony that circled the entire golden
dome. I gulped, unwisely looked down, and saw just how
far above the city we were. This was almost as bad as
flying across the city in an Asura's talons.

Thunder crashed above us and made me jump. In
all the excitement of solving the labyrinth of the palace,
I had forgot about Mahishasura's deadly storm. I
grabbed hold of the balcony rail and held on for dear
life. Ashwini laughed, giddy with delight that we'd
actually made it up here. 'We're almost there,' she said.
'We're nearly free!'

I craned my neck all the way up and looked for the

gandaberunda. It loomed above us on top of the ridged dome, a glorious golden statue at least twice my size. This version of the mythical eagle, which I had based on the one that's still a part of the emblem of the real Mysore, had two heads, enormous folded wings and three emerald eyes. The fourth eye was a golden jewel.

The statue must only have been about six feet above my head, but it seemed very far away. There were no stairs on the balcony, no ladder, no easy, convenient way to scale the rest of the dome.

I was going to have to climb.

And then the thunder abruptly stopped. The skies cleared. A pale-gold sunrise winked down at us.

This seemed like good news at first, but it wasn't.

'Kiki,' Ashwini said, much too calmly. 'Start climbing. *Now.*'

I turned, just in time to see her draw her sword. My skin prickled. 'They're coming, aren't they?'

'Don't look,' said Ashwini. She shoved a sheathed knife into my hand so that I could use the blunt end to break the golden jewel. 'Just get to that statue as quick as you can. I'll hold them off.' Her jaw was set, her hair fluttering in the wind. She had never looked more heroic. 'Go, Kiki!'

I don't want to say goodbye, I wanted to tell her. *Now that we're here, it's too soon. I want more time with you.*

But there was no time to waste, and she'd done so much to get me here. I couldn't fail her now.

So I shoved the knife into my pocket and started to climb.

The ridges of the dome gave me somewhere to put my hands, but the marble was slippery. My hands shook and I forced them still. The smallest mistake would send me hurtling to the ground and that would be the end of me *and* of any chance we had at breaking the gandaberunda's eye.

Slipping and scrabbling at the marble, I pulled myself up, bit by painful bit. The wind whipped my ponytail into my face and I had to spit it out of my mouth before I could keep going.

'You're almost there!' Ashwini called up to me. 'You can do this, Kiki! You can fix this for all of us!'

Somewhere else, much too close, I heard the shriek of an Asura. I shuddered and my hands slipped, but I snatched at the base of the statue and latched on just in time.

I pulled myself up and balanced on the gandaberunda's clawed feet. The statue was silent, waiting. Four stern eyes looked down at me, sparkling in the sun. If I stood on my toes and stretched as high as I could, I would just about reach the golden eye.

'Hurry!' Ashwini shouted. 'I can't protect you while you're up there!'

I reached for the knife in my pocket and then put one hand on the statue's chest. It was warm, warmer than I'd ever believed gold could be, and I could have sworn I felt the soft, quiet pulse of a beating heart.

Unable to stop myself, I looked back over my shoulder. Some distance away, hovering in the air, was a huge bird Asura, a mixture of vulture and crane. It let out another shrill cry. As its enormous wings slowly rose and fell, its vicious eyes were fixed not on Ashwini and her sword on the balcony below, but on me.

Wait.

Why wasn't it attacking me? What was it waiting for?

Again, under my hand, I could feel the faint, persistent heartbeat of the gandaberunda. I hesitated, one hand on that heartbeat, the other holding the sheathed knife so tightly that my knuckles had gone white. It seemed utterly wrong to destroy the eye of the creature whose heart I could feel humming right there under my hand.

'Kiki, what are you doing? You're running out of time!'

But the Asura didn't come any closer.

I could still feel the heartbeat, a little fiercer now.

'Kiki!'

I had to move. I had to do this. It was our one chance. I had to keep Mum safe. I couldn't let her down the way I had let Pip down.

Suddenly, all I could see was Pip in his final moments. His chin tipped up, his face full of defiance, so totally and utterly *alive*.

He wasn't any more, but he had been. He had been *so* very alive. Jojo and the twins, and even Lej, they were all alive. Ashwini, right below me, was alive. And Simha and Chamundeshwari and the other people of this city, and even the Asuras themselves, they were *all* alive. What did it matter that they had come from my sketchbook? What did it matter that none of this was *meant* to happen? It *had* happened. They had been transformed and now they lived, they breathed, they were *real*. And if I broke the gandaberunda's golden eye, if I unmade this world, then none of them would be alive any more.

I hadn't been happy about doing this for a few days

now, but it had seemed like the only way. No, it had seemed like the *easy* way. Brahma had insisted on it, but Vishnu had told me to fight Mahishasura, and *that* had been too terrifying, too impossible, so I'd let myself believe Brahma's way was the right one.

I'd had a choice, and I'd chosen this.

But it wasn't too late to choose differently.

I let the knife slip out of my hand and listened to it clatter down the slope of the dome. Then, with one final look at the gandaberunda, I followed the knife.

'*Good,*' the palace whispered.

As I found my footing on the balcony once more, Ashwini's eyes blazed furiously at me. 'Why didn't you do it?'

'I couldn't,' I said. 'I know it was the easy way, but I couldn't do it.'

'*Why?*'

Tears filled my eyes. 'You're all so alive. I know you said you were never supposed to be, that none of this was supposed to be real, but it *is*. I'm sure it would be easier for me if I could just go home and pretend this world was only ever just a bunch of stories in a sketchbook, but I can't do that. Like it or not, this world *is* real, and so are you and the Crows and the hundreds of other people who live in it, and I won't just undo all that. That *can't* be the right answer.'

'What about your mother?'

'I don't know,' I said, a lump in my throat as I thought of her. 'I'll keep her safe. I won't let them win. I don't know how I'll stop them, but I will.'

Ashwini opened her mouth, but then her eyes darted over my shoulder and her lips set in a line. 'I told you to stay at home,' she said, but not to me.

I turned and, much to my surprise, saw Lej step out of the window. His face was hard and cold. I had never seen him look so furious, which, frankly, was saying something.

'How did you get up here?' I asked, astonished.

He gestured to something shiny on his back. It looked like a peculiar metal backpack at first glance. 'I flew,' he said. 'Right into a window on the top floor, where I saw you two climb out of *this* window.'

I was so distracted by the revelation that he'd actually found someone who could build him wings, or something like wings, anyway, that it took me a second to notice the furious look on his face was gone.

'You didn't do it,' he said. 'You could have been

home with your mother by now, but you stayed. You saved us instead.'

'I lost Pip,' I said, my voice breaking on his name. 'I'm not losing the rest of you.'

Ashwini scowled at Lej. 'Why didn't you stay at home?'

He scowled back. 'I think you know why.'

I looked skittishly out at the Asura in the sky, still close, still a threat. 'Can we go back inside? The palace will keep us safe if any of them try to follow.'

'We don't have to do that,' said Lej. He sounded kinder, which made me realise that, for once, it wasn't *me* he was angry with. 'The Asura won't attack us.'

Ashwini scoffed. 'Why not?'

Lej's voice was bitter. 'It hasn't attacked yet, has it? Kiki came *this* close to breaking the gandaberunda's eye and it didn't even try to stop her. Why not?'

My knees wobbled. My brain was always so crowded and noisy that I hadn't been able to pay attention to the important stuff, but the moment Lej's words sank in, all those small, important clues came rushing out of the dark corners. Like how a demon king imprisoned the one person who could banish him rather than kill her. A set of keys dropped outside a locked cell. An empty fortress. A locator spell that was never used. An eye that had to be broken. Thunder. An Asura that hadn't attacked.

They were little things, not much on their own. But when I put them together, what I saw was that I had been twisted and turned like a puppet. Each of those little things had been a nudge down one specific path, to get me all the way to this moment, to right here.

I swallowed. 'The Asura didn't attack me when I climbed up to the gandaberunda because it *wanted* me to break the eye.'

'Don't be ridiculous!' Ashwini burst out. 'Why would it have wanted that? If you'd broken the eye, they would have lost everything!'

Mahishasura's first words to me came rushing back. *Such a small girl*, he had said. *To think that you made this world, and hold the keys to my way out of it, and yet you cannot even look me in the eye without trembling.*

He had said it to make me feel small and helpless, and it had worked, but that wasn't what I felt now. Now I could think only of the little bit in the middle, a tiny piece of information he had probably never meant to let slip: I held the keys to his way out of this world.

'He would have been free,' I whispered. I felt sick.

Lej nodded. 'You worked it out quicker than I did.' Had he been anyone else, I would have said he sounded impressed, but he was Lej, so the odds were very much not in favour of that.

'We made a mistake,' I said to Ashwini, whose face had turned to stone. 'If I had broken the eye, this world would have collapsed back into ink and everyone who had come here from somewhere else would have been sent back to their own world. Like me, and like Mahishasura. We assumed he would be sent back to the Nowhere Place, but that's *not* his world. *My* world is his world. And that's where he would have gone. He would have got exactly what he wanted.'

'You don't know that,' she said.

'We *all* know that,' Lej snapped.

'Wait.' I looked between them with growing horror. 'Why would Brahma want me to do this? He must have known what would happen.'

'Brahma never wanted you to break that eye,' said Lej.

'But he said—'

I stopped abruptly, one hand flying over my mouth. Because I understood, at last, what Lej was getting at.

What if Brahma hadn't said anything at all? After all, only one of us had ever talked to him.

'No,' I choked out.

'Do you know where she was before the storm?' Lej asked me. 'Last night, after everyone went to bed, Simha saw her sneak out of the house. He was worried, so he followed her. She went to Lalith Mahal. She went in, right past the guards, like she'd been there before. And when she came out, he said, the storm started.'

I looked into Ashwini's eyes. They were dark and defiant, a stranger's eyes. 'You knew what would happen if I broke the eye,' I said. 'You knew the whole time.'

And she said, 'Yes.'

26

'I've never met Brahma,' said Ashwini, letting out a breath as if it was almost a relief to tell us this. 'He wasn't the one who told me about you and the sketchbook. It was Mahishasura.'

There was a dull, painful roar in my ears, the sound of my heartbeat and my noisy brain and the wind all at once, and I felt like everything was being ripped out from under me. Everything I had known, everything I had trusted, was crumbling. She was the one who had been with me right from the beginning; the one who had appeared in London with her gleeful grin and her bravery and her fondness for cookies. She had been my friend. I'd trusted her. She had saved me, and I had saved her, and we'd taken almost every step of this weird, impossible adventure together.

How was it possible that none of that had been real? How was I supposed to reshape everything I remembered and believed to fit this new, ugly picture?

There was a horrible lump in my throat. 'Everything you told me in London was a lie. Everything you told *everyone* was a lie.'

'It was easy to pretend Brahma had asked me to come and find you,' she said. Her face was flushed, as if she was embarrassed or maybe even ashamed, but her voice stayed clear and defiant. 'Who could contradict me? Didn't you ever wonder why the tear between worlds wasn't guarded before you got here, but was afterwards? Mahishasura didn't want you to be able to go back, speak to Brahma yourself and find out the truth.'

I couldn't believe it. I didn't *want* to believe it.

I could feel the sting of tears in my eyes, but I made myself speak. 'Y-you've been helping him the whole time I've known you?'

She gave me a small rueful smile. 'If it helps, I'm not happy about it. When Mahishasura discovered that the tear had opened up on a page of your sketchbook that featured just me and one of his Asuras, he knew only we would be able to cross over into the real world. So he found me and convinced me to help him. He said he needed you. As the architect of this world, you were the only one who could break the gandaberunda's eye and free him. You were also the only one, we assumed, who could get past the palace traps. So the Asura and I broke out of your sketchbook, had that dramatic fight in London, and then I convinced you to come back here with me.'

'And the other fight you had, with Mahishasura and the demons in the street?' I asked, my voice unsteady. 'That was faked?'

'Of course,' she said. She sighed. 'Then Vishnu turned up, which was unbelievably inconvenient, and I was sure you'd find out the truth the moment you told him you'd been asked to break the gandaberunda's eye. But he didn't want to listen to you, so you never got to tell him. And then you came up with the idea of the Good Witch.'

'That's why you wanted to break her out of the fortress,' Lej said furiously. 'You knew it would be easy. You told Mahishasura that Kiki needed her, so you knew he would let us take her.'

'That was just a distraction,' said Ashwini, waving a hand. 'I never actually planned on going to the fortress.

The moment Kiki found out about the Good Witch's locator spell, I knew she'd go back to the tear sooner or later.' My face flushed with shame, and with fury that she'd deliberately used the mess inside my brain against me. 'When she did, Mahishasura's minions were waiting to capture her.'

'And then Mahishasura let me escape with the Good Witch,' I finished for her.

'What about Pip?' Lej growled.

For the first time, Ashwini's expression cracked. 'He wasn't supposed to go with her,' she said. I remembered her horror when we came back, the way she had stood there and said, 'This should never have happened' over and over. 'Even after he got himself captured, too, he was supposed to escape with Kiki and the Good Witch. But then Mahishasura ...' She looked down at her hands.

I clenched my hand on the balcony rail. My heart felt so bruised and sore that I didn't know how to cope with it.

'And then the storm,' said Lej.

She looked up and nodded. 'He didn't want to wait any more. He pretended to try and rip the tear between worlds wider, but he just conjured up a lot of thunder. The point was to make Kiki feel like she was out of time. It worked,' she added with a faint smile. 'You got here, didn't you?'

'But *why*?' I hated how desperate my voice sounded, like I needed her to give me a reason that would somehow make all this OK. 'Why would you help him? He's a monster!'

Her eyes flashed. 'Yes,' she said bitterly, 'he is. He's the monster *you* forced me to fight.' In a rush, the words that must have been bottled up for so long came tumbling out. 'Look at what you did to me! An Asura slayer? What a life to be stuck with. I had to fight monsters. I had to look after all the others. I had to be *tough* and *brave* all the time. I never got to be a kid, or to have fun. I never got to be scared or fall apart. I couldn't, because there was no one to look after me. I had to *fight*, no matter what. And the worst part, of course, was that I could never have won. None of us could have beaten him. We were doomed to fight and fight and fight with no way out.'

'*He* did that, Wini,' Lej protested, the nickname as heartbreaking as it was unexpected. '*He* made us real. Kiki never wanted any of this to happen.'

'But he gave me a way out,' she said. 'He told me that I could try to run away as soon as I crossed over to

278

the real world, but if I did that, he'd kill all of you. But if I helped him escape, he promised me that he would take me with him. I'd be able to have whatever life I wanted in the real world. I would be *free.'*

'While the rest of us became ink and paper,' said Lej hoarsely. I noticed, for the first time, that there were tears on his face. He was devastated.

Guilt turned Ashwini's cheeks red, and her eyes were wet, too. 'I couldn't do it any more,' she said, pleading with him to understand. 'I couldn't keep being the one everyone depended on.'

I couldn't bear it. 'I'm sorry. I'm so sorry. You're the one who has to live with the choices I made, so I get why you hate me. I do. And I don't blame you.'

She stared at me like she hadn't expected that. Then she bit her lip and said more quietly, 'I want to hate you, but I don't. What I said to you last night, about how there's nothing wrong with you? I didn't say that because I was playing a part. I want you to know that. That was real. There were a lot of times when I pretended to be your friend, but *that* wasn't pretend.'

Somehow, that almost hurt more. I didn't know how to make sense of someone who had been real and false at the same time.

'*How* you *felt was real,*' the palace said quietly. '*None of it was pretend for you. You can trust that.*'

I looked up from my cold clenched fist on the rail. Ashwini and Lej were both watching me. 'I made it so easy for you to lie to me.'

'That's not a bad thing,' she said. 'You're kind and you care, which is why you were so easy to trick. Lej certainly helped me make you feel guilty, even if he didn't know it,' she added, and Lej flushed red. 'You didn't have to come here, but you did. You wanted so badly to fix the mess you'd made. You shouldn't be ashamed of that.'

I tried to speak, but the lump in my throat had grown too hard. I wrapped my arms around myself, exhausted and cold and crushed. The grief and hope and betrayal of the past two days were too much.

Eventually, I asked the question I dreaded most. 'So what now?'

'You have a choice, Kiki,' said Ashwini. 'You can break the gandaberunda's eye right now. Or you can refuse and Mahishasura will find a way to force you.'

'There's nothing he can do to force me,' I said, teeth clenched. 'After what he did to Pip, I'll *never* help him get back to the real world.'

'We both know that's a lie,' said Ashwini. 'If he

threatens to hurt your mother, you'll do whatever he says.'

'He can't get to her!'

'*I* can,' she said, looking me straight in the eyes.

I didn't believe she would do that, or maybe I just didn't *want* to believe she would do that, but the fact that she had even said such a thing made me want to shake her until her teeth rattled. 'I'll stop you, and I'll stop him.'

'How?' she asked gently. 'With a sword you don't know how to use? With a bow you can't fire?'

'I'll find a way,' I snapped. 'And you? What are *you* going to do if you can't get out of here?'

She shrugged. 'I don't know. I guess I'll find a way, too.' And then, with one last small smile, she said, 'Good luck, Kiki. Maybe one day we'll meet again.'

As she said the words, she whirled around. Lej, obviously sensing what she was about to do, leapt forward, but he was too late. With one last look over her shoulder, Ashwini jumped over the balcony rail.

'No!' I shrieked.

Lej grabbed me around the waist to keep me from throwing myself at the rail. 'Kiki, don't!' he said, yanking me back. 'She knows exactly what she's doing. Look!'

I saw the bird Asura from the sky swoop down, so quick it was not much more than a blur, and a moment later it flew up into the air with Ashwini safe on its back. I watched her until she vanished into the blue.

She didn't look back.

'We should go,' said Lej in a low voice. As I wiped my wet cheek with the back of my hand, I saw him do the same thing to his face with his sleeve. However heartbroken I felt about what Ashwini had done, he had to feel worse. 'She'll tell Mahishasura what happened. He'll turn this city to dust just to force you to break that eye. We have to stop him.'

I let out a ragged, incredulous laugh. 'You say that like it'll be easy.'

'You know, I was up here for a while before I let you see me,' he said. 'I could have come out sooner and warned you not to break the eye.'

'Why didn't you?'

'Because I didn't need to. I knew you wouldn't do it.' This was perilously close to an actual *compliment*, so I just blinked at him, shocked, and he went on, 'Just like I know now that you'll find a way to win.'

'You do remember that you've spent almost a week telling me the exact opposite?'

'Yes. And that was unkind of me.' He scuffed his shoe awkwardly on the balcony floor. 'I'm not very nice to anyone, but I was much worse to you. I know I told Ashwini just now that this was all Mahishasura's fault and it wasn't fair to blame you, and that's true, but I did blame you at one point. I hated that you'd given us these lives. I hated that you got to be a kid with a mum who loves you while we lost our families and our childhoods.' He looked up at me. 'I guess I convinced myself that everything that had happened to us was all just fun and games to you. So that's why I was pretty horrible to you. Then we had that argument before you got captured, and you told us why you created all this. I realised it *wasn't* just fun for you. You cared.'

'And then Pip died,' I said gently.

'Yeah. And I lost my temper.'

I did some of my own awkward scuffing of shoes. 'Pip would still be here if it wasn't for me. You don't have to feel bad about what you said to me.'

'Pip died because Mahishasura is evil,' Lej said. 'That's the *only* reason. I should never have said it should have been you instead of him.' His voice cracked and he brushed a hand over his eyes. 'He was my favourite. All he ever did was try to make people happy, and he tried twice as hard for me. When I saw what happened to him, something inside me just broke. It wasn't fair to take it out on you.'

'It's OK. Honestly.'

'Thanks.'

Another awkward pause. We were *really* bad at this.

'For what it's worth,' he said after a moment, with the briefest of grins, 'I don't actually think your rainbow unicorn pyjamas are silly, either. They're kind of OK.'

'Careful,' I said. 'You could hurt yourself displaying such unbridled enthusiasm.'

'Shut up.'

I smiled as I stepped back into the palace. 'Now *that* sounds more like you.'

27

I don't know what we expected when we got back to Crow House, but the mess and Suki's inconsolable sobs were not it. Our arrival only added to the mayhem. Jojo burst into tears, Suki threw herself at Lej and Samara raced over to hug me.

'You came back!' Suki cried.

Lej took a step back and stared hard at her. 'Why wouldn't I come back?'

'We th-thought you m-might have left us, t-too,' she sobbed.

Lej looked shocked, and a little hurt. 'I wouldn't do that. I promise.' He looked around. 'Ashwini was here, then?'

'Yes,' Simha rumbled from the corner, where he

was lying beside three empty teacups. 'She told us what she did.'

'She asked us to go with her, to join Mahishasura,' Jojo added, scrubbing at his face with his sleeve. 'She said if we didn't, we'd end up like Pip and she didn't want that. She said we would *all* be able to go back to Kiki's world if we helped Mahishasura win. We said no.' His voice wobbled and he gestured to the mess around the front room. There were shreds of black, red and gold everywhere. 'She said she couldn't believe we were turning our backs on her after everything she'd done for us. Then she tore up all our costumes and left.'

I knelt down beside his wheelchair. He had a pile of the fabric scraps on his lap. 'I'm so sorry, Jojo,' I said. 'I know how hard you worked on those costumes.'

'It's not that,' he said. 'It's what she said. It was like *we* had betrayed *her*.'

It was Lej who said firmly, 'That's not true. She loves us, but she's hurt and she made a bad choice. That's on her, not on us.'

'It *is* our fault, at least a little,' Suki said unhappily. 'I was always asking her for stuff, and Pip and I were total nuisances, and we all just needed her so much all the time. I don't think I can blame her for wanting to leave us.'

'Well, I can,' said Lej. 'We should have helped her more, and asked a whole lot less of her. Believe me, I know that. But none of that makes what she did OK.'

'But, Lej,' said Samara, her voice small, 'what do we do now?'

I could tell Lej didn't have an answer, but that he wanted to give her one. With Ashwini gone, he was the one they turned to. But he looked very young all of a sudden, and I found myself coming to his rescue.

'Plan B,' I announced.

'What's Plan B?'

'We fight him,' said Lej. 'Right? We go to battle.'

I nodded. I swallowed back my doubt and my fear, and I said, 'Simha, Chamundeshwari has been gathering people to come and fight with us, hasn't she? That's what Vishnu asked her to do.' The lion nodded his great head. 'OK, then we'll get them all together. Anyone who'll fight with us. We'll ask the Good Witch to help, too. And we'll all go to Chamundi Hills, just like in the old story, and we'll meet Mahishasura outside Lalith Mahal. And there, one way or another, we'll stop him for good.'

No one said that there was no way we could win, but we were all thinking it. No one pointed out that Mahishasura's army would overwhelm us in no time at all, but we all knew they would.

No one said any of that because even though we knew we'd probably be defeated, we still had to try. Because there was a chance, because we owed it to Pip and because we all deserved a life without the monsters.

'OK,' Lej said at last. 'That's what we'll do.'

'We won't have our costumes,' Samara said sadly.

'We don't need them. We still have bits and pieces of armour.'

'I know we don't need them,' she said. 'It's just that, they were *us*. You know? They said we were a team, that we were a family. I know it's silly, but they made me feel braver.'

I understood. It was like my statue in the square outside. I had made the bold, brave, strong version of myself that I had wanted to be, down to the superhero pose and cape, because sometimes when you put your shoulders back and put on a cape, you feel like you can do *anything*. Costumes are a small thing, but as Pip showed us over and over, something small can make a big difference.

I looked at the tragic shreds of black, red and gold fabric in Jojo's arms and all over the floor. Ashwini must have hacked at them with her sword because they were beyond repair. And there was no time for Jojo to make new ones for everyone, even if we all helped.

Then I remembered a bird shaking itself loose and flying into the sky, and my hand closed over the broken piece of my pencil in my pocket.

'Maybe I can help,' I said.

They stared at me, but I didn't explain. How could I explain it, anyway? Better to show them.

I started laying shreds of fabric out on the floor, like puzzle pieces. After a moment of bewildered silence, the others started to help, with Jojo directing which shred should go with which specific pile, and eventually there were several mostly complete jigsaw puzzles of fabric on the floor of the front room.

Then I picked up my pencil and started to draw.

I drew lines between the shreds on the floor, like pulling a jacket zip up, and everywhere I drew the lines, the fabric *merged*. Suki gasped, and Jojo's eyes went wide. I sketched line after line and filled in any gaps and holes with smooth strokes of the pencils that Samara fetched for me. And I watched with as much amazement as the others as, one by one, torn pieces of costumes became whole.

When it was done, I knelt on the floor while the others stood around me, their jaws slack. Seeing all his hard work repaired, Jojo looked like he might start crying all over again.

'Extraordinary,' said Simha.

'How did you *do* that?' Samara asked, using the same awed whisper she had used that first day when she saw me at the door and said, 'It's you!'

'I don't know,' I said honestly. 'I didn't know I could until yesterday. It's not much,' I added quickly, fully aware that a few costumes wouldn't win any battles, 'but I hope it makes you feel better.'

'Oh, Kiki,' she said, hugging me.

'But where's *your* costume?' Simha wanted to know.

'Well, I didn't think—'

'Don't worry,' said Jojo, grinning, 'I've been working on yours for the past couple of days. I can finish it in an hour.'

'But I—'

'Stop it,' Samara said. 'You're part of this family, too.'

Lej shook his head in amazement. 'I was wrong about you,' he said. 'It doesn't matter that you can't aim an arrow or use a sword. You have your own kind of power.'

And Suki, at the sunlit window, said, 'Little girls are always more powerful than people think we are. People think we're sweet, precious things, all sugar and spice and everything nice, but we've got iron and steel in us, too.'

I looked down at the broken pencil half in my hand, thinking of little girls and monsters and power. An idea started to take shape in my mind.

'You have a look on your face I don't like one bit,' Lej said in the doomed tone of someone who can see a storm coming and knows he's about to be swept up in it.

'Um,' I said slowly, a smile inching across my face, 'I think I know how we can beat Mahishasura for good.'

Over and over, I had been told I was just a little girl, but there was no such thing as *just* a little girl. The Crows had helped me see that none of us were *just* anything. I didn't have to be what anyone else said I was, I didn't have to fight my battles the same way as everyone else, and I wasn't going to let anyone keep me quiet and scared any more.

This was *my* world.

And it was time to take it back.

28

I knelt at the window in Ashwini's bedroom for what could be the very last time and took a long look at my kingdom. It had been a magical, joyful place once and I knew that I could make it that way again.

I could see it in my mind, bright and vibrant like a page out of my sketchbook: where the dust drifted over the rusty tracks, there would be a merry red train chugging across the city; where the fairground stood empty, there would be a circus, cotton candy and laughter again; everywhere you went, you'd smell mangoes and dosas and fresh Mysore pak; the silent, dark forest would sing with birds; the jewel houses would be filled with loud chatter and windows would be thrown wide open; magical chariots would fly the

Crows up to the pastel castle; and no monsters would ever block the light of the sun again.

It was possible. I had to believe that, that a world that had gone dark could be bright again.

In the distance, I could see the golden and red domes of Mysore Palace. And the gandaberunda at the top, silent and still.

'Wake up,' I whispered. *'Please.'*

There was no answer. The statue didn't stir. Why hadn't it woken, like the legends promised? How could this *not* be Mysore's time of greatest need?

'It will wake when it's ready,' Chamundeshwari's voice said from behind me. 'This world is a part of you, Kiki, and the gandaberunda is a part of you, too. Trust in it.'

I turned. She stood in the doorway, her braid over her shoulder, a white sling around one arm. The Good Witch was with her.

'You came!'

The Good Witch rolled her eyes. 'Does a sun shrew live for a thousand moons?'

'That's a yes,' Chamundeshwari translated with a small smile. 'I reminded her that you freed her from Lalith Mahal. It was the least she could do.'

'And what is it you wish me to do?' the Good Witch asked, looking very put-upon.

'A spell,' I said. 'If I were to make a few hundred small things, could you turn them into a few hundred *big* things?'

She squinted at me suspiciously. 'Yes.'

I grinned. 'Then I'd better get to work.'

Armed with the coloured pencils and ink Crow House had given me, I shut myself up in the front room downstairs and started drawing.

I drew for hours, ignoring the ache in my neck and hand. Over and over, I traced the same shapes a hundred times, then two hundred times. The sun crept up in the sky and the day grew hot and sticky as the others came and went with drinks and snacks and conversation, but I kept drawing.

'Do you have a minute?' Jojo asked at one point, poking his head in the doorway. He wheeled himself inside. My finished costume was on his lap.

I could have squealed. It was my very own superhero costume. Like the others' uniforms, it was a full stretchy suit in black with red-and-gold panels across the chest, hips and around the cuffs of the sleeves and legs. The gold sparkled with stardust and moonbeams, an extra bit of protection from teeth and claws.

'It's *perfect*,' I said. 'Thank you.'

He grinned, thrilled with himself. 'You can try it on later,' he said, and gestured to the drawings on the floor. 'I'll let you get back to it.'

I went back to it.

And then, just as I finished my final piece, there was a tremendous shriek in the sky outside. It rattled the windows and shook the walls, and my skin prickled with goosebumps. It was high and shrill, the cry of a bird when it sees a threat, and it echoed across the entire city.

Suki burst into the room. 'Kiki, it's happened! It's really happened! The gandaberunda is awake!'

It was time.

29

We marched across the city to Lalith Mahal. We were a pretty magnificent procession, if I did say so myself. Chamundeshwari rode at the front on Simha's back, a glorious goddess with a golden spear in one hand. Lej, the twins and I followed, with Jojo and the Good Witch right behind us in a shiny mechanical chariot that I had sketched for them before we'd left.

And we weren't alone.

As we made our way down the streets, around the corners and up to the long white chariots' driveway in front of Lalith Mahal and Chamundi Hills, Asuras watched us from the sky. Like a storm, they gathered, throwing shadows across us, waiting to see what we would do. By the time we reached the white road,

Mahishasura and the rest of his army had come out to meet us.

They spread out in front of their gleaming white palace, hundreds of monstrous demons, with horns and teeth and claws. There was no sign of Ashwini, of course. She had said a pretty final goodbye at the top of the palace.

Mahishasura stepped away from his army. He was even bigger in the full light of the sun than I remembered, muscled and tall, horns sharpened, with nostrils puffing and those amber eyes narrow with malice. He searched our faces, stopping when he found mine, and I watched him take in the costume, the colours, the small sword in my hands. I swallowed hard, suddenly certain that this wouldn't work, that I'd been foolish to even try this, that everyone I loved – in *both* worlds – was going to pay the price for my stupidity.

He crossed his arms over his armoured chest. 'What is this?' he boomed across the distance between us.

'This is the end, Mahishasura,' said Chamundeshwari. 'It is time to finish this.'

He snorted. 'You are merely a pale imitation of the

goddess who banished me,' he said. 'What makes you think you'll do any better than she did?'

'It is not I who will conquer you,' said Chamundeshwari gravely.

I took a step forward, then another. 'I will,' I said to Mahishasura. 'I want to fight you, *just* you. One fight.'

'Why would I bother with such nonsense when I could just defeat you and all your companions in battle?' the demon king demanded. 'You are hopelessly outnumbered.'

'Are we?'

There was a clank of steel behind me and I saw Mahishasura's eyes dart over my shoulder. I knew what he could see: a goddess, a lion, a witch, four kids and over a hundred of the brave ordinary people of Mysore. There were familiar faces in the crowd, too, like the old man with the coconuts, the witch from the black market and the woman who swept the square outside Crow House every morning.

And behind them all, marching out of the streets on to the driveway like a flood, were three hundred soldiers in black, red and gold.

What Mahishasura didn't know, of course, was that the soldiers weren't real. They were just toys – small tin soldiers I had spent all day sketching to life in the front room of Crow House, and the Good Witch's spell had made them human-sized. They could march with us, and stand with us like an army, but they would crumple if they were attacked. They couldn't take on a horde of Asuras.

But they didn't need to. They just needed to make Mahishasura hesitate.

Another shriek split the sky in half. Mahishasura's head snapped up and his amber eyes widened as an enormous silhouette swooped out from behind the clouds and circled over us. The gandaberunda's wings were so huge that they almost blocked out the setting sun. Talons raked the air and four bright jewel eyes glared down at the demons. And the demons, rather sensibly, took a step back.

'I think we can win,' I said to Mahishasura. I didn't try to hide the way my hands were clenched white around the sword, or the tremor in my voice. I didn't care if he knew I was afraid. In fact, I *wanted* him to know it. 'But after what you did to Pip, I don't want anyone else to get hurt. So if I can end this one-to-one, just you and me, I'd prefer to do it that way.'

'What foolishness has possessed you to make you

think you can defeat me in battle?' Mahishasura scoffed. 'Did you not listen to anything I told you? Look at you! You are no match for me.'

'If you're so sure of that, you have no reason to turn me down.'

His eyes burned into mine, cold and calculating. 'And what are the terms of this fight?'

'The first person to bring the other to their knees is the winner,' I said. 'If I beat you, you go back to the Nowhere Place. If you beat me, I'll send the gandaberunda back to the top of Mysore Palace and break its golden eye.'

'How do I know you'll keep your word?'

'How do I know you'll keep yours?'

I could see him mulling this over, those teeth clenched. Then a huge bison demon rumbled from behind him, 'The girl cannot possibly beat you in a fight, my king. She is every bit as foolish and conceited as every other human, so why not use this chance to teach her a lesson?'

The Asuras stirred, obviously very keen on the idea of teaching a silly little girl a lesson. Mahishasura's pride couldn't resist it.

'Very well,' he growled. 'I accept your terms.'

I nodded. My hands were sticky with cold sweat, but I gripped the sword tightly and took another step forward, then another, until there were only a few feet between the demon king and me. He didn't pick up a weapon of his own. I guess he didn't need one. His claws and teeth were all he needed to tear me down.

'You may strike first,' he said generously. Behind him, his hordes snickered.

So I struck first. I heaved my sword up and swung it uselessly in his direction. He batted the blade away with the back of his gauntlet. Laughter snorted out of his nose and he didn't bother to strike back. When he'd cornered the Good Witch, Pip and me inside Lalith Mahal the other day, blocking our escape, he'd told us that he had fun watching us scurry around his fortress like frightened mice, so it came as no surprise to me that he didn't try to finish our battle quickly. It was more amusing for him to watch me humiliate myself.

He let me strike, over and over and over – futile, pathetic jabs with a sword I could barely lift off the ground. After all, I was not a natural warrior. I was, in fact, an absolutely terrible warrior.

'Is this supposed to be our evening entertainment?'

Mahishasura taunted me while the horde of Asuras howled with laughter. 'You cannot even hold that sword properly! And you think you can win?'

I wanted to tell him that yes, I *did* think I could win, and I was in fact *going* to win, but the words died in my throat. What if this didn't work? What if I had made a big mistake? Was it too late to back out? If I stuck to this plan and I failed, I would cost everyone *everything*.

Stop it, a voice in my head said. It sounded a lot like Ashwini. *You're obsessing again. And that's OK, but you need to see it for what it is.*

I could do this. The terrible thoughts were inside my head, not out here. Maybe they would always be there, but I could see them for what they really were now.

I can win, I said silently. *I am* going *to win. And I'm going to do it my way.*

Out of the corner of my eye, I saw Suki. Her teeth flashed. *Little girls can beat big bad wolves. We have teeth, too.*

Teeth weren't all the same. For so long, I had made the mistake of thinking we all had to fight monsters with the same weapons, but that wasn't true. The

Asuras had their claws, Chamundeshwari had her chakra and Ashwini had her sword. And mine?

Mine was mightier than any sword.

So I dropped the actual sword on the ground, sobbed and ran.

Behind me, Mahishasura's loud, surprised boom of glee shook the trees. 'Look at her!' he cried. 'Fleeing like a rabbit!'

His army joined in with a cackle that spread like ink in water. Until, out of nowhere, Suki's voice cut across them.

'You haven't beaten her,' she called, loud and clear. 'Those were the rules. You only win if you beat Kiki.'

Mahishasura growled. 'She ran away. She loses by default.'

'Um, she's still out there, isn't she?' I could picture Suki pointing at my back as I fled, just as we rehearsed. 'If you haven't beaten her, you haven't won. So why aren't you chasing after her?'

Silence.

And Suki giggled. 'Huh. I guess you're scared.'

Mahishasura let out a snarl, but unlike Pip, who hadn't had anyone to protect him, Suki was behind Simha, Chamundeshwari and the other Crows. Mahishasura couldn't take his fury out on Suki, but I knew he wouldn't be able to bear the idea of anyone thinking he was afraid of me, a weak little girl. So he did the only thing he could.

He chased me.

As I raced past the gargoyles and back towards the city, I looked back once. The Asuras in the sky swooped and the gandaberunda met them with a vicious slash of its talons. The demons on the ground leapt forward. Simha seized one around the throat and flung it to the side. Chamundeshwari's chakra sparkled as it flew into the heart of the Asura army.

I turned and kept sprinting onwards, away, into the city and down the empty main street to the palace at the other end.

'You cannot hide inside your maze of traps, Kiki Kallira!' Mahishasura thundered behind me, so very close. 'I will find you no matter where you go!'

I let out another loud sob and kept running towards Mysore Palace. Past the gates, down the overgrown grounds, until I stumbled to a halt under the tallest arch. Above me, carved into the marble, two words shone in the sun.

'Never terrified,' I whispered.

'*You are braver than you think,*' the palace whispered back. '*And stronger than you know.*'

'Are you OK with what I'm about to do?'

'*Yes.*'

Trembling, I turned back to face Mahishasura. 'Leave me alone!' I shouted. I threw in another whimper for good measure. 'I don't want this any more! I just want to go home!'

His eyes gleaming maliciously, Mahishasura advanced. I backed away. His body bent into a crouch, the final move of a predator before it pounces on its prey, and I fled along the row of columns to the botanical garden.

This time, the palace didn't need me to prove myself, so it helped me. Trees shifted, shrubs jumped aside and there wasn't so much as a mechanical spider leg to be seen. I ran unhindered across the maze. Behind me, the maze shifted to make things just a *little* harder for Mahishasura, but still let him pass.

I burst into the palace ballroom and raced for the stairs. Mahishasura followed, his horns tearing tapestries off the walls as I crossed the grand entrance hall. As soon as I hit the second floor, I bolted for the library.

As I ran, my hand closed over my pencil and I started to use it. I drew a crack here, a fissure there, deep crevices on the marble walls and floors, until the palace started to tremble around me.

In the library, between two shelves crammed with dusty, beautiful books, I found the hiding staircase with a piece of rainbow thread tied around the bottom post.

I raced up the stairs. Mahishasura was on my heels, his breath hot on the back of my neck.

I opened the door at the top of the stairs, and threw myself into the room beyond it, where the walls were lavender and white. Backing away from Mahishasura, who snorted smoke from his nostrils and chuckled at the sight of me cornered in a room, I watched as the door behind him closed.

And vanished.

Because this was, of course, the Room with No Doors.

'No way out now,' I said, shrugging.

As the walls quivered around us, the palace groaning with broken stone, Mahishasura's teeth bared in a snarl. 'What have you done?'

I watched as it dawned on him, bit by bit, that he had been tricked. He had been so utterly certain that I was just a scared little girl, he had found it entirely believable that that little girl would demand a fight and then run away in tears. He had so completely underestimated me, he hadn't even paused before following me into the palace I had made and only I could get out of.

'You think you have lured me into a neat little trap,' he growled, his fur simmering with heat and fury. 'You think you are strong and clever, but you are not. You are a scared, lost little girl, Kiki Kallira, and you will never be more than that.'

I backed away some more, until I collided with the wall behind me. 'If that's all I am, why haven't you beaten me yet? I think it's because you've always known, just like I know now, that I have more power in this world than you ever will.'

'*I* am the ruler of this world!' Mahishasura roared. 'You will never win. If I am trapped here, so are you. You will never be free of me!'

'My real battle was never with you,' I told him. 'It was *you* who helped me see that. My real battle was with the version of me who was afraid of herself. My real battle was with the version of me who let people like you make her feel small and weak. And, as you can see, I've already won that battle.'

And then, with the immense satisfaction of having had the last word, I drew myself a new door, slipped through and sealed it shut behind me.

30

I ran. I had to get out. To be absolutely sure that no one would ever let Mahishasura out of his prison, I'd left all those cracks in the walls and the floors. The palace was about to come crashing down.

'*Faster,*' the palace whispered, as I sprinted across the ballroom.

There was a rumble like thunder behind me as the earth itself quaked. I didn't look back. I pushed my way across the maze as trees and hedges parted seconds before I reached them. I ducked under the arches at the front of the palace, avoided the falling columns, and ran down the overgrown thorny path until I got to the gates.

Out of breath and holding on to one of the gates to keep myself upright, I turned back. There was a final *crack* and the palace collapsed like a house of cards. Dust exploded outwards, columns snapped, towers crumbled and I covered my ears to try and block out the cataclysmic roar.

When the dust settled, I saw that the palace had not been destroyed – it had been transformed! The marble and stone had reshaped themselves into a single tall column. One dome remained and now sat at the very top, a new perch for the gandaberunda to keep watch over Mysore. The palace had gone, but in its place was a monument. It was the colour of honey and sunsets, and it marked the place where Mahishasura was buried for ever.

'You're still here,' I whispered. 'You're still *you*.'

And the palace didn't answer back, but I could have sworn I felt something brush my cheek, like a loving grandma saying goodbye.

I couldn't move for several minutes. My heart was still pounding so fiercely that I couldn't stop trembling. I couldn't quite believe what I had done.

My plan had *worked*.

I had beaten Mahishasura.

I had saved my golden kingdom.

As silence crept over the now empty grounds and

the minutes passed, I became aware of sounds and movement in the nooks and shadows of the city around me. Whispered voices, cautious footsteps.

One by one, people crept out of the streets and took tentative steps on to the grounds. Their faces were all turned towards the monument, their mouths open with awe and their eyes wide with fear, shock and something that looked a lot like hope. Then, slowly, all those eyes turned to me.

One woman took a shaky step forward. 'Did *you* do that?'

I nodded, unable to speak.

'Is he gone?'

I cleared my throat and forced my voice to work. 'Yes.'

There was stunned silence.

Then, before anyone could react, Suki burst from the nearest street and rushed towards me, her face glowing with glee. 'Kiki!' she squealed. 'Kiki, you did it! You won't *believe* what happened on the battlefield! The demons were winning, but then the palace collapsed and everything went quiet. It was like the moment Mahishasura died, every Asura felt it and the battle just *stopped*. And then Vishnu appeared and the Asuras scattered because I guess they knew that with Mahishasura gone, there was no one to protect them from the power of a god. A few of them escaped into the forest, but Vishnu banished the rest into the Nowhere Place. Then he told us that you had won and Mysore was saved and so we ran—'

'Kiki!' Samara gasped, appearing over Suki's shoulder, out of breath. 'Are you hurt?'

'No, I don't think so,' I said, so relieved to see them. 'Are you? Is anyone else?'

'We're all fine,' said Suki. 'Simha, Chamundeshwari, the Good Witch and the gandaberunda kept the Asuras from totally swarming over us, so we got really lucky. Lej and Jojo are on their way here.' She threw her arms around me. '*Thank* you!'

'You don't have to thank me—'

'Yes, we do,' Samara insisted.

'And I owe you an apology,' said a voice.

I jumped. Vishnu had appeared out of nowhere, tall and stern and strong, his dark eyes glinting in the setting sun. At the sight of him, the crowd around us let out a collective gasp.

'I doubted you,' Vishnu told me, which was an understatement if ever there was one. 'I belittled you and diminished you. I was wrong. You have proven several times over that you do not need my respect or my approval, but know that you have both, nevertheless. This is the end of Mahishasura, and the start of a better future for all worlds, and we owe that to you. Well done.'

And then, with the smallest of smiles on his stern face, he bowed his head and vanished.

31

If I had hoped that beating a monster and saving a kingdom would be the end of it, I would have been very disappointed because, as it turns out, there's a *lot* to do after you win a war. A bunch of people wanted *me* to be the new queen of Mysore, but a lot of other, more sensible, people felt it should be Chamundeshwari, who was a grown woman and a goddess and was not about to go back home to London.

Still, it was a *little* disappointing to pass up the opportunity to force Lej to address me as, 'Your Majesty,' but we all agreed in the end that Chamundeshwari was the better choice.

Simha decided that he would live at Crow House for good, so that someone over the age of twelve was around to look after the kids, but this was only settled after Suki made him promise never to cook again. The Good Witch turned my tin soldiers back into toys. And the gandaberunda took its place at the very top of the tower and became just a statue once more.

No, not *just* a statue: it was Mysore's protector, always waiting, always watching, ready to wake when the city most needed it.

None of us talked about Ashwini. Her betrayal had crushed me, but I'd only known her a few days, so I knew that the others, who had loved and depended on her for years, felt much worse. And I didn't want to think about her being all by herself, either, somewhere out there in this kingdom of ink, monsters and magic. Was she sorry? Did she wish she could come home? Was she OK? I didn't know if I would ever be able to forgive her, but I did know that, even now, I cared too much about her not to worry about where she was and whether she would ever be happy.

I had no reason to stay in Mysore any more, but I didn't want to leave. Not yet. Not until I got to see it get its happy ending.

I knew I couldn't make all the pain and fear disappear just because the monsters were gone, and I knew it would take time for the people of the city to recover and build new, better lives, but there were a few things I *could* do.

So I went out into the city with pencils and the Good Witch's spells. I fixed broken houses, painting them over with whatever bright new colours the people living inside them wanted. I rebuilt the train. I wiped away the scorched earth where Mahishasura had burnt the farms and redrew new ones, with new crops and new orchards, so that there would always be food for everyone. I drew the circus back into the city.

And, bit by bit, noise and joy and magic came back to one small pocket universe, tucked safely inside a little girl's sketchbook.

As for the Crows, I drew gifts for them. New figures and cards for their *Giants & Gargoyles* game, a grand library for Samara, a greenhouse for Suki, a sewing machine for Jojo, an enormous teacup for Simha so that he wouldn't have to drink out of tiny human ones any more and, for Lej, a pair of his very own rainbow unicorn pyjamas.

He made a spluttering sound when he opened the present I'd neatly wrapped and tied up with a bow. And then a smile crept across his face.

'They're great,' he said.

'I know,' I said, and grinned back.

'I still don't like you,' he warned. 'Well, not all that much, anyway.'

'Don't worry, I feel the same way.'

From across the square, where she was exploring her sunny new greenhouse with giddy delight, Suki shouted, 'You know, you didn't have to give us presents! You did save us, after all.'

'I couldn't have done any of it without you,' I said. 'All of you. And if you don't believe me, let me tell you how I got to the top of Mysore Palace ...'

So I told them, about Jojo's glamour jacket, Samara's apple, Suki's freezing potion and Pip's stink bomb.

'You see?' I said, when I was done.

Lej gave us a slightly crooked smile. 'I don't think I played a part in any of that.'

'Are you kidding?' I said in disbelief. 'Who brings Jojo the stuff he uses to make costumes and clothes? Who buys the seeds Suki needs? Who finds the books, the swords and all the weird things Pip must have used to make that stink bomb? And who,' I added, 'flew up to the top of that palace with only a pair of very odd, dubious wings just to warn me about Ashwini? You were a part of all of it, Lej.'

Before he could reply, from somewhere inside Crow House, Simha's voice boomed out: 'WHY IS THERE CAKE ON THE TABLE? WHAT DID I SAY ABOUT SUGAR?!'

At last, I couldn't put it off any more. I had to go home.

On my final night in my golden kingdom, there was a party in the square, with music and fireworks. Crowds of excited people turned up to dance, thank me and give me heaps of extremely delicious food (my favourite of the three).

At the very end, before the fireworks, I stopped for a second and looked up at my marble statue on its plinth. There she was, the heroic Kiki I had once wanted to be. I still didn't know if I was like her. I would never be the kind of girl who saved the world with cool superpowers or battled monsters with swords, but those were not the only ways to be a hero. And I knew now that I *was* brave, and I *was* strong, in my own way.

Maybe I would always fight with my own brain, and maybe I would always be a little anxious and a little afraid, but there was nothing wrong with that. And when I went back to London, I'd talk to my mum and she'd help me and, one way or another, I'd be OK.

The sun had started to climb up the sky when the twins, Simha, Chamundeshwari, the boys and I broke away from the party and made our way to the tear between worlds. By the time we got to the balcony of the tall house on Pretty Corner Market, the sky was pink, the rest of the city was awake and Suki had started to bawl.

'I'm going to miss you,' she cried.

I hugged her, then each of the others in turn. 'I'll miss you, too. All of you.'

'Even Lej?' Suki demanded.

I looked at Lej, who looked deeply suspicious at the idea of a hug. 'Even Lej,' I admitted.

'Come back if you can,' he said, much to my surprise.

I was about three seconds away from bursting into tears that would rival Suki's, so I quickly nodded. 'If there's a way, I'll find it,' I promised them.

The crack between worlds was in the corner of the balcony, a small slash of bright light that hummed with energy when I got close to it. I looked back one last time at the six faces behind me.

Then I stepped into the little tear of light—

And tumbled out on to the floor of my bedroom.

The first thing I noticed was the cold. Had it always been this cold in London?

I clambered off the floor and looked around. At the window without curtains. The pencils and pens strewn across every available surface. The tin Ashwini had taken a few cookies out of. The slightly crispy blankets and open sketchbook on the floor. Outside the window, I could hear the honk of a distant car horn, the muted voices of people coming home from a late night out, the rattle of a train far away.

More than a week had passed for me, but no time at all had passed while I'd been gone. It looked like that was one thing Ashwini hadn't lied to me about.

I could hear Mum above me, rolling over in bed. I wanted to rush up the stairs and hug her, but I resisted. There'd be time in the morning.

There was a sudden noise behind me, the violent flapping of wings and then a quiet thump.

I spun back to my sketchbook. There was a bird flying around the room, bumping merrily into the walls and letting out little caws of glee.

'Did you follow me back here?' I asked incredulously.

The bird hopped on to my windowsill and cocked its head at me. Its eyes twinkled.

It hit me, suddenly, that it wasn't just a bird. It was all black, with a little gold on its beak.

It was a crow.

And that twinkle in its eyes …

My voice cracked. 'Pip?'

The crow winked.

Throat tight and heart racing, I reached out a hand. But before I could ruffle the crow's feathers, it opened its beak and nipped my thumb.

'Oi!' I protested, bursting into surprised laughter.

Definitely Pip.

I picked up my sketchbook, where the tiny crack glowed weakly, and then, with a flicker, it vanished like it had never been there. I ran my hand over the spot where it had been. A fat teardrop fell on the paper, but I wiped my eyes and flipped through the book.

There had been several blank pages in my sketchbook the last time I had looked at it, but now it was full. There were new sketches in colours so vivid I could have sworn they were alive: a witch in a white fortress, ashes on a river, a two-headed eagle soaring across the sky, a girl and a demon king inside a room with no doors ... and a crow.

I had given my Mysore a happy ending, but this wasn't the end of *my* story. This was more of a happy middle for me.

'Are you going to stick around for a little while?' I asked the crow.

With a little caw and a shrug of its wings, the crow found itself a nice nest on top of a pile of books on my windowsill, and went promptly to sleep.

I got into bed, burrowed under a spare blanket and held my sketchbook close, thinking of the story it told, of the world inside that I had to keep safe.

The crack between the two universes was gone, and I didn't know if I would ever be able to cross between worlds again, but I could hope. Maybe my adventures in my Mysore weren't finished. Maybe I'd find a way to go back. Until then, I'd live my own story.

So, for now, I said goodbye to that other world. And closed the book.

ACKNOWLEDGMENTS

Where do I start? With my parents, who taught me that stories are as necessary as cake, sleep or air? With my grandfather, who gave me endless gifts of folklore and adventure? With my husband, who makes it possible for me to hide away in a quiet place and write books like this?

Well, I guess I've started with all of them. But they're not the only ones who made this book possible. So here, then, are a few other thank-yous:

To my smart, ferocious agent, Penny Moore, who fights for me, cheers me on and pushes me to be better than I think I can be.

To Jenny Bak, my brilliant editor at Viking, whose passion for Kiki's story has been boundless. Thank you for making this book better every time you take another look at it.

To the rest of the incredible, supportive team at Viking: Aneeka Kalia, Delia Davis, Abigail Powers, Mia

Alberro, Aliza Amlani, Krista Ahlberg, Kelley Brady, Kate Renner, Kaitlin Kneafsey and Ken Wright. Working with you all has been such a joy and privilege.

To Kate Agar, Aliyana Hirji and the rest of the wonderful team at Hachette UK. Thank you so much for bringing *Kiki* home.

To Nabi H. Ali, for the gorgeous cover art. Thank you for bringing Kiki to life!

To Jem, Henry and Juno, for reminding me to laugh.

To Freyja, Caitlin, Tilda, Maisie, Evie, Sasha, Sabina, Olivia and all the other little girls who prove, every day, that there really is no such thing as *just* a little girl.

Finally, to you. Thank you for sticking with Kiki, and with me.

Love,

Sangu